DOWN HIGHWAYS IN THE DARK...BY DEMONS DRIVEN

Dan Henk

To
Monica
Henk
My late
wife
who always
believed in
me.

DEADGUYLLC

Productions

Down Highways in the Dark...By Demons Driven Copyright @Dan Henk. All art by Dan Henk.

Tall Tales

BY DEMONS DRIVEN

INTO THE WILD

I t all started when I was 14 and ran away to New York City. Away from North Carolina and my super-conservative, "spare the rod and spoil the child" father. He had whipped my ass for the last time.

Didn't he understand that it just made me hate him and his "holier than thou" attitude? What did he know? He believed the world was six thousand years old, that dinosaur fossils were really the bones of fallen angels from the war in heaven! Or maybe Satan just put them there to make the real believers question their faith!

But I was talking about my trip to New York. I was hanging out at the usual getaway, the side of a dusty road that was all sunlight and baked asphalt. Some long-haired hippy, or headbanger-I was too young to tell the difference-pulled up in his car. A rumbling polished black '60s Mustang that made me wonder why anyone bought anything else.

The door cracked open, and flashing a crooked smile, the driver beckoned me inside.

I was a little deviant-sporting shoulder-length blond hair and outfitted in a faded "Ride the Lightening" T-shirt. But this guy looked way more advanced in my chosen subculture. Greasy locks poured down to his waist, commingling with square jawed, Clark Gable good looks. All the girls must have loved him, and all the guys probably wanted to be him. Although I didn't know it at the time—I just thought it was strong incense—the interior reeked of weed.

"Hey, man... where you headed?"

His drawl was thick.

"I... New York City."

"Hop in. I'm going up to Syracuse."

I knew you weren't supposed to take rides from strangers, but my own dad had picked up hitchhikers before. And this guy looked, I don't know, cool.

"You coming? I ain't got all day."

I mustered up my best pretense.

"Yeah, man. Thanks."

He halfheartedly ran the standard questions by me.

"Why you headed up to NY?"

Accompanied by the unspoken implication.

You sure I won't get in trouble for this?

I was quick on my feet, and rather than blurt anything out, I slowly unwound a story more or less made up on the spot. It included my super religious military dad, the ass-whooping I had just received, and a little bit of extra embellishment about him

kicking me out. I exaggerated details of my beating and received the sympathetic

"Yeah, man, that shit sucks."

Even the cursing struck me as cool! I'd get my ass kicked six ways from Sunday for doing that in the house. The windows were rolled down, a cascade of wind gushing in. Pulling out a pack of Winston reds, he yanked open a well-used ashtray and started to light up. I debated whether I was pushing my luck, but managed to a croak out a-

"Hey, man, can I get one of those?"

He gave me a funny sideways glance.

"You sure you can handle it?"

"Sure, I smoke all the time."

I tried to sound smooth and relaxed as I lied through my teeth. He shrugged his shoulders, pulled out a stogie, and casually dangled it in my direction.

"Thanks. You got a light?"

With the first puff I got an instant head rush. We rolled on in silence as I breathed in the warm afternoon air and felt that all was right with the world.

"Hey, man, open that glove box."

Startled, I responded with a hazy,

"What..."

Instantly I felt like a retard. I was hoping he wouldn't notice the redness in my cheeks, when he followed it up with-

"This silence is killing me. I got some cassettes in there."

"Oh."

I felt even more stupid and popped open the glove box. After rifling through the cassettes, I caught sight of what looked like a gun handle. I tried not to be too obvious, but he was already a step ahead of me.

"Can never be too careful, huh? I think I have some Slayer in there."

I was used to guns. It was my dad's hobby—collecting guns and shooting things. But this felt a bit weird. Awkward and rebellious even. It was a .45 semi auto by the looks of it, and that was a pretty serious firearm. I wondered for a minute if he was a criminal.

A bank robber on the run, with a trail of death and chaos behind him!

"*Hell Awaits, I think. You ever heard it?*"

That broke me out of my reverie.

"*Yeah, man, I love that album!*"

I had picked it up from the used tape shop a few days earlier, although I wasn't sure if it was my thing yet.

"*Yeah, good shit. Pop it in.*"

It started with a low grumbling, mounting into the sounds of hell and just as it was about to reach a crescendo, the thrash guitars came charging in. That's when everything seemed to click.

Thundering down the road to the steady throb of a V8, a cigarette dangling between my fingers, the breeze blowing through my hair, the warlike strum und drang of the guitars. Little did I know how fleeting that feeling would be.

THE BIG CITY

Day had faded into a dusky night by the time we reached DC. I had never been to the city, but the glossed over tourist photos of an idyllic capital were a total lie.

"Hey, man, you wanna see something cool?"

The driver (funny, he never did tell me his name) had diverted into the city. We were now rolling through what I would later find out was Southeast. It looked like Hell on earth. Vacant lots housed the dregs of society. They were roughly swaddled in stained clothing, their weathered blankets sprawled out and only partially obscuring the grimy terrain. Styrofoam cartons and the detritus of a fast-food society were strung all about, further staining land that was beyond all hope of reclamation. Abused shopping carts rested caddy-corner on the chewed-up remnants of sidewalks, some of them trailing a stream of tattered clothing. Battered brick buildings surrounded us, the blacked edges of ashy sills jutting out. And the stares... like we were subhuman invaders, trespassing on their territory. Their eyes glared at me from beneath darkened cowls, insinuating that I didn't belong. I sunk lower into the seat, feeling very young and out of my element.

"You scared?"

I hadn't heard from him in a while, and the sound startled me.

I was definitely scared.

"Ha-ha! Don't worry. See, this is where that gun comes in handy!"

The light just ahead was changing to red. A wave of terror washed over as we rolled to a stop.

"Hand me that gun."

"What..."

I was hoping he wasn't serious, but he glared at me with eyes cold as ice.

*"I said **Hand me the fucking gun.**"*

A bead of sweat rolled down my temple. I popped open the glove box and slowly pulled out the gun, handing it over grip first. He snatched the .45 out of my hand, immediately turning to the open window and gesturing wildly at the people outside. Every nerve in my body tensed up, and I tried to shrink down further in my seat.

"You guys know what this is?"

The bystanders just gave him a look like they had guns waved in their face all the time. The light changed, and with a laugh, he handed me back the pistol, punched the transmission into drive, and peeled out. That's when I first thought twice about this whole adventure. When awe for his perceived hipness turned into regret. But the rest, the rest wasn't really his fault.

NEW YORK CITY

It was well past dark by the time we approached the outskirts of New York City. We had stopped at a 7-11, and I was slowly nursing my heavily sugar and cream laden coffee, something he found endlessly amusing.

"You gonna have a little coffee with that sugar?"

I had now polished off three whole cigarettes, and my mouth felt like an ashtray. It didn't help that the caffeine was surging through my body, making me antsy.

"So, where we dropping you off?"

His voice struck me like a megaphone. In my caffeine-fueled concentration, I had zoned out, and hadn't even noticed that the tape had ended miles ago.

"You do have a plan, right?"

"Oh, course... of course... Just drop me downtown,"

I had absolutely no plan and was already regretting this whole thing. I was a little kid alone in New York City. I didn't know anyone here.

"Where downtown? Times Square? Union Square?"

"Umm... I--"

"You don't fucking know, do you?"

"No, no... Times Square!"

I was feeling trapped and wanting off this ride! At least I'd heard of Times Square.

"Ha, you better watch your little Southern ass there. Lots of perverts running around."

That made me shudder, and the way he had referred to my "little Southern ass" didn't help.

"I'll be fine. I know somebody there."

"What, in Times Square? Nobody lives in Times Square! Except maybe Travis Bickle!"

"Who?"

"Never mind."

I avoided his gaze and stared out the window. The city looked a thousand years old. A massive labyrinth of stone and iron, the edges all soiled with what I imagined was the wear of centuries. The dark holes of windows scaled skyward in twisting ramparts that dissolved into the smog as they ascended. Everything at ground level was barred and shuttered. Steel gates were drawn over the entrances accompanied by massive padlocks that secured them in place. This felt like something out of a movie. We rounded a bend, and a blazing panorama of sparkling lights greeted us. Neon billboards exclaiming XXX! Peep Show! Sex Shop! People that resembled horror movie extras wandered about. Girls strutted the streets in skintight outfits, their breasts popping out like ice cream scoops. What little skin was clothed was wrapped in outfits more outrageous than anything I had seen on MTV. Silver. Shiny red. Sparkling gold. Clear high heels. Big hoop earrings. Makeup that resembled war paint.

"This is what you wanted, right?"

I almost refused to get out, debating whether it was safer to stay in the car with a known evil or venture outside into an unknown one. I glanced over, and my driver was staring at me. I decided that if there was one thing I wasn't, it was chicken-shit. I mustered up my nerve and climbed out.

"Thanks for the ride."

He stared at me for a moment, shook his head, and peeled out. I watched the car grow steadily smaller in the distance, too afraid to look at anything else. It made it through a light, narrowly missing a black guy yelling curses after him, and disappeared around a bend. A breeze kicked in, the airborne remnants of a newspaper assaulting my legs. I realized it was getting cold, and goose bumps sprang up on my arms. I ran my hands over them in an attempt to stay warm.

"Well, what do we have here? "

I swiveled around and was face to face with what I surmised was a Hispanic guy. At least I thought he was Hispanic. His olive face was swathed with greasy black hair, the edges tumbling out from under a gray fedora. His face was partially carpeted by dark stubble, and he was dressed in a white tank-top held up by black suspenders. I had never seen anything like it, but his sneer was terrifying.

"I... I..."

"You lost, kid?"

"No... I..."

"You a runaway?"

I didn't want to tell him the truth. He was a grownup, and in my naive mind, they were all connected. Not only that, but he looked like a villain from a *Crocodile Dundee* or *Indian Jones* movie. I didn't know what to do, so I just turned and ran. Bounding down the sidewalk and leaping a curve, a taxi blared loudly as it swooshed by me. Another car, coming from the opposite direction, bore down on me, and I made another running jump. Landing on the sidewalk, my right knee buckled, but I managed to right myself and awkwardly scramble forward.

"Fucking kid,"

I heard somebody yell. My temples pounded, my eyes peeled wide, and I peered around desperately looking for any way off the streets. The streaked glass windows in front of me sported colored circles with bold, black letters. I recalled them being the trademark of New York's famous subway. That suspicious guy was still staring at me from across the street. I caught a glimpse of a silhouette disappearing into the building beside me and figured that must be the subway entrance. I headed for it.

As I rounded the curb, a small cluster of half walls opened into a descending stairwell.

Was this the subway?

A skinny black guy came around the bend, not even looking at me as he hustled up the stairway. I had never seen a haircut like his before. Except on TV. I remember it being called a "high top fade." He looked urban, hip, and like a character from another world. Almost everyone on base had short hair, military short, and their clothing was much blander. Even his shoes looked sharp—all brown polished leather, and way classier than the usual combat boots I was used to.

I darted down the steps, figuring they probably led to the subway. As I passed the man shot me a curious glance. His eyes opened wider as I passed, and I imagined I could feel the burn of his stare but didn't dare look back. Around the corner a row of metal turnstiles stretched out before me. A glass-paneled booth stood guard on the left, a shadowy figure just behind. I then realized I needed money if I expected to get on the train.

Shit!

I had $20 I'd stolen out of my mother's purse, but that was for essentials. Food and cigarettes! I peered back over my shoulder. There were no signs of pursuit. Yet. I glanced about feverishly. A guy popped around the corner behind me, and for a moment my heart stopped. Then I saw it wasn't the creepy guy, just some swarthy white guy. Loud female voices broke out. Two women—ladies of the night, I was to later learn—came around the bend. Glossy short dresses, one gold, one pink, sky-high heels, and with soft mountains of breasts spilling out of tight tops. The one in pink was white and had frizzy blond hair, the black roots at least an inch thick. The other looked Spanish, with an almost identical haircut, only raven black. A slight mustache graced her upper lip. The girls were giggling, talking over each other, and didn't appear to be in their right state of mind. Giant hoop earrings flashed as they talked, their heads moving in rhythm with the words. I heard a thump, followed by cursing. Spinning around, I saw that the white guy was pounding on the glass of the kiosk, shouting obscenities at whoever was inside. Taking this as my opportunity I ran, vaulting the turnstiles and not even bothering to look behind as I continued down the steps.

OUT OF THE FRYING PAN...

About half a dozen shadowy forms were milling about below. A few glanced my way, the more benign looking ones staring at the pavement. The two that noticed me looked rough. A black guy in a thin red leather jacket and a Spanish guy sporting a Yankees cap. Both wore a quiet look of disdain as they craned their heads toward me. They exchanged a few words I didn't catch. A weary looking man with a mop of brown hair, hands buried in a well-used Carhart jacket, stood near the edge of the platform. He leaned over to peer down the dark tunnel as the black guy yelled at him.

"Whatcha lookin for, faggot?"

He didn't respond, just craned his head a little more, and stared more intensely down the yawning gap.

"I said... whatcha looking for, faggot? What, you deaf or something?"

The black guy wandered over casually, the Spanish guy snickering and uttering something too low for me to catch. I was about midway in between, but it felt like the guy was coming right at me. Trying hard not to look, I took turns staring at the distant wall and my feet. I backed away slowly, hoping the approaching guy wouldn't notice. When I looked up, he was almost in front of me.

"Don't worry, kid. I got nothin' on you."

I wasn't even sure what that meant, but at least I wasn't the target.

"Hey, faggot, got a light?"

The black guy was getting close now. Hands still dug in his pockets; the other guy was peering down at the tracks. His drooping jowls, garnered by an oily, stubble-dotted face, seemed to radiate a sense of resignation.

"I said..."

Suddenly the guy spun around, whipping out his hand to reveal a snub-nosed revolver.

"You want some of this? Is that it?"

"Whoa, whoa... I was just asking for a light, buddy..."

"I'm not your buddy. I don't smoke. I know how this game is played. You think I'm stupid? Is that it?"

"You trippin... I'm not playing any game."

"Oh, yeah? Then how bout you just head over there. "

He gestured at the far pillar.

"You and your friend can look for the next easy mark, cause it ain't gonna be me."

Just then, the train whistle sounded, and a gust of air burst forth. The man with the gun caught the brunt of it, stumbling forward a little. In an attempt to correct his footing, he stepped back too far and missed the ledge. Just as the train came rushing into view. He almost made it.

Everything happened so fast, the edge of the train catching him, spinning his body around in a mad twirl as gravity pulled him down. The tight confines between the ledge and the train sandwiched his lower extremities, the sidewalls of the train repeatedly striking his upper body and twisting him like a pretzel. He didn't even cry out but his mouth fell open in shock. The train screeched to a halt. Someone was yelling, and beneath it all I could hear the thump of footsteps. Everything slowed down, the shadowy forms of transit workers, emerging out of the peripheries. The black guy staggered back, mouth agape. And then, like some grotesque abomination, something that should not be... the trapped guy spoke.

"Help... help me... somebody..."

An EMS worker surged past and was quickly joined by another.

"Sir. Is there anyone you want to call? Family members? A priest?"

The worker was kneeling, his expression painfully earnest.

"I'm just... I'm just stuck..."

"Sir, your injuries... They're life ending."

"No, really, I'm just... just stuck... If you move the train..."

"The moment we move the train, you will die. Your body has been ground to pulp."

"But I... I'm not in pain... I just feel numb..."

"That is because your spine is broken."

"But I..."

"The train is acting as a tourniquet. The moment we move it you are dead. Your body is shutting down as we speak. You need to tell me if there is someone we can contact."

The man's expression withered, and he started to cry.

I had never seen an adult cry before.

I looked away, paralyzed by shock. A moment or two passed—it felt like ten minutes, but it could have been ten seconds—and when I glanced back, a tear-streaked, lifeless face stared at me.

"That's it. He's gone."

The EMS worker stood up and headed toward the front of the train.

I couldn't take my eyes off the dead guy. It was horrifying. I felt nauseous. My eyes were watering, my legs turning into rubber. Then he spoke.

OH, WHAT A SHALLOW LIFE WE LEAD

"This wasn't supposed to happen... I'm not ready to die..."

My mouth dropped, and I stared at his face. His cold, unmoving face.

"Kid... you can hear me! I'm still here... somewhere... I just can't feel my body... You gotta help me..."

"I... I..."

I started to stumble backwards.

"Kid... please... I got no one... I'm from Romania... I..."

Reality started to fade, and everything went dark. I felt a warm, reassuring hand on my shoulder. Out of the corner of my eye I saw a young black woman in EMS garb mouthing words to me I couldn't hear.

I woke up in a bed I was later to learn was in Bellevue Hospital. My body was swathed in a white hospital gown, its faded blue flowers shimmering faintly in the cool light. I sat upright and looked around. Pale blue curtains hung from walls of pipe. Through a slit in the curtains, I saw signs of movement. Someone nearby groaned and rolled over. The curtains parted, and a pretty, dark skinned young woman with extremely white teeth stepped through. I liked her smile.

"Hey, Aaron, we feeling better today?"

How did she know my name?

"Uh..., sure..."

I didn't know where I was, what time it was, or even what day it was. I tried to piece together the last things I remembered, and suddenly it came surging back. The black guy. The guy with the gun. And the incident...

"Your parents are here, Aaron. If you're ready, I'll bring them in."

My heart sank.

My parents! How did they find me! What was my dad going to do?

But he didn't do anything. He was oddly soft-spoken too, barely even making eye contact. My mom was there, too, and kept shooting me disapproving glances.

"Aaron, we're going home now. Get dressed."

I glanced around and saw that my clothes were neatly folded on the bedside chair. I looked up and my dad was glaring at me. His face registered no emotion, but I could sense something akin to anger. I felt naked and exposed in the thin hospital gown. Quickly climbing down, I scooped up my clothes and practically flew around my dad as I looked around for a bathroom.

Should I run? What chance did I have in this big city? I doubted I could get a job, and I didn't have any place to stay...

A sharp rap on the bathroom door snapped me to my senses.

"Are you ready yet? We have a long trip ahead of us."

It was a long trip. My face burned, and I felt angry and ashamed. A couple of times I caught my mother shooting me daggers. I tried not to meet her gaze. My dad didn't kick my ass like I thought he might. In fact, he didn't even talk to me for days. My mom continued with the steady withering looks, the whole incident slowly fading with time. I had nightmares. Fantastical dreams that replayed different versions of the incident. More often than not, it would be the part where that guy had just pulled out the gun. I would run toward him, trying to give a warning. Usually, he didn't even take notice. It was like I was invisible, the interplay between him and the other guy a forgone conclusion. A few times he noticed me, spinning around, the barrel pointed at my face. At that point I would wake up, drenched in sweat and gasping for air. On rare occasions, the guy shot me. I heard it, and saw it, but felt no pain.

Over time, the whole thing started to fade. Then it happened again.

THE INEVITABILITY OF FATE

Two years passed, and we moved from North Carolina to Northern Virginia. I was heavy into punk rock by then. Sneaking out at night, stealing the family station wagon, and hitting the shows at the 9:30 club downtown. There was a punk shop on M street called Smash, and I hung out there all the time. I could rarely afford to buy anything—it was all overpriced and cheaply made—but I'd flip through the singles, looking for something cool and obscure. Usually, I made it down there only on weekends, but it was my seventeenth year, I had just lost my job at Elie's Deli for mouthing off to the spoiled sister of the owner, and I had nothing better to do. It had cost nearly all my money, taking first the bus and then the train into the city, but there was a cool, hip allure to downtown. I could walk for hours down M street. People would stare, shooting strange looks at my blue hair and painted leather jacket, but I didn't care. Sometimes the more ghetto kids or douche-bag jocks would shout stuff. I'd hurl insults back, hopping on my skateboard and cruising away before they could pursue me. On one such occasion a couple of jocks had asked me if I was a faggot, and I told them to ask their mom. They gave chase, and I took off down the side streets. Whipping around corners, disapproving hisses and grumbles were cast my way as I narrowly avoided the startled pedestrians.

I had made it to Tenth and K. Walls of corporate hell jutted up all around, the swarming mass of straight-laced society flowing past. A lanky black guy in tight yellow and black spandex sped by. A bike messenger no doubt.

Then, so abruptly it was as if it materialized out of thin air, a city bus hurtled out of the traffic. There followed a deer-caught-in-headlight moment, and the huge side walloped the courier. He flew over the handlebars, the bike quickly sucked under the tires. Clearing the corner, he smashed headfirst into the side road and rolled into an unconscious, prone position. People stopped in mid-stride and started to turn; their reflexes slowed by shock. One guy, all buzz cut and navy business shirt, started running toward him. The bus rounded the corner. Everyone could see it coming. Hands were flung upward. Warnings were shouted. But it all happened so quickly. And just like that, the bus rolled over him.

His head burst like a melon. Tires screeched. People shouted. Brakes squealed. Everything became a blur. A cluster of suits pressed in, the transient crowd of a business day. I managed to wiggle through the throng as a voice in my head warned me that anything I saw would scar me. After all, I hadn't been able to sleep for weeks after the incident in New York. But I couldn't help myself.

Just as the crowd thinned enough for me to catch a glimpse, I knew I had seen too much. Jagged chunks of skull lay scattered about. Pink on one side, a few pitiful cornrows still clung to the other. A crimson-speckled goo bubbled out of gashes in the mangled flesh. Blood bathed the street and underside of the bus. I leaned over, hands on my knees, trying not to retch.

Civilized authority came rushing in. Men in official looking blue uniforms. I stumbled back toward the steadiness of a concrete wall. My vision blurred at the edges, and I was breathing deeply. Then, clear as day, a voice popped into my head.

"Fuck, man!"

I opened my eyes so fast that a new wave of nausea hit me and I had to grip my knees.

"I can't be dead. That can't be me! This some shit dream or somethin'!"

There was a pause.

"Fuck, man! Fuck! Fuck! Fuck! What do I do now? I got a wife at home. We got a kid on the way."

A cold sensation gripped the back of my neck.

"What do you want?"

Was I imagining it?

My eyes wide, I peered around but the mob paid no notice.

"Hey, kid... You can hear me?"

"Kid, what's going on? Where am I?"

The dizziness was intensifying. I just wanted everything to go away. And suddenly it did. So rapidly I fell to my knees and started heaving. I'd had nothing for breakfast except coffee, so there was only a burning liquid coming up.

"It'll be all right."

I felt a hand on my shoulder and looked up. The sun rendering him only a silhouette, I could tell by the voice that it was an older man. My vision was swimming, but he looked strangely dressed.

"You hear them, don't you?"

"Wha... what?"

"The dead."

"Is that... but, how do you..."

"They aren't completely dead, you know. Just in this dimension. But it takes a very special boy, just like you, to hear them. Come with me. I have an office near here. It'll get you out of the sunlight and give you something to drink."

He helped me to my feet. My throat burned, and I felt out of sorts. I loped forward and he steadied me enough that we made it around a corner. An old, battered door came into view. He produced a key and opened it. Within, pale light gleamed down a wooden staircase. I shook my head, trying to clear my head.

As we reached the top, a wooded door embedded with a large monolithic paned window greeted us. He unlocked the door, and ushered me in. A clustered jumble spread out inside. Filing cabinets topped by a disarray of yellowing papers, an old Underwood typewriter nestled atop one.

What was this place?

I saw a stool and headed for it. I needed to sit down, gain my bearings. The man seated himself in a chair nearby. Dim light permeated air saturated with floating motes of dust. I looked up, blinking to clear my vision. He resembled a movie star from days past. Square jaw, dark hair, and piercing blue eyes that were barely visible under the brim of his hat.

"You know you have a gift?"

"I... you mean what I hear?"

"Exactly."

"Everyone has this ability, but few can access it. It's an evolutionary region that has long since reached a dead end. But genetics is a gamble. You never know quite what is going to be activated."

His words and tone were reassuring, but still, something, I don't know, something seemed off.

"I know this is probably difficult, but you can't speak of it. The normal, everyday word fears what they don't understand. A couple hundred years ago, they would have

lobotomized *that part of you they thought gave voice to demons.*"

He let his words sink in for a moment.

"*I'll give you my card. We'll talk more about this later. I'll get you some water.*"

With that he rose and disappeared around the file cabinet. My head was clearing a little more now.

Was he crazy? Should I run? Maybe this was all a dream, like one of those old Twilight Zone episodes.

"*Here you go.*"

I almost jumped!

How did he get right beside me so quickly!

Accepting the water, I realized I was suddenly parched and took a hearty swig. Cool and slightly sweet. I emptied the glass and set it on the desktop.

I felt a little better, my head clearer. Then I fell over.

THE MORNING AFTER

Waking up in my bed, I threw the pillow aside and wrestled off the covers. I was still in my hoodie and my feet hung off the side. My whole body felt hot and swollen. I slowly sat up and looked around. I was in my downstairs bedroom, festooned with Frank Frazetta and Misfits posters. The windows were covered by heavy shades, but sunlight still made its way in. I groaned and gripped my head. My left arm hurt, and I rubbed it absently. Standing up, my legs numb, I stumbled toward the door. A random glance at my drawing table revealed a card. I clicked on my art lamp and picked it up. Scrawled with tight, small ballpoint lettering it announced, "the man you met yesterday" followed by a 202 number. I flipped it over.

Paranormal Studies

ESP

Agent 7

999 K Street

I smirked at the address.

Was that intentional? Bad joke if so.

Pocketing the card, I cracked open the door and peered out. All was silent, no trace of my mom or dad. I tried to think.

Was this Saturday?

It had been Friday when I headed down to Georgetown. Ever since the last time I was almost expelled from school, my classes had been cut down to three a day, so it had been easy enough to cut out early on Friday. I popped into the downstairs bathroom and flipped on the light. Whoever had lived here before us had painted it lime green. Edging over to the counter, I pulled off my hoodie and held up my left arm, rotating it slowly. On the backside were two clotted holes, about the size of a small nail head. I pushed at them gently and there was some deep bruising. I shook out my arm and headed out.

I could see sunlight shining through the sliding glass door downstairs, bathing the couch and TV in a pale blue glow. I noticed my dad and mom were sitting on the couch and almost jumped! The newscaster caught my eye. Dan Rather, I think, and he was frozen, like someone had hit pause on a VHS.

"Mom?"

She didn't answer.

"Dad?"

Again, no answer.

"Hello?"

I slowly rounded the couch. Their eyes were open, a casual look on their faces. My mom's eyes were directed at the screen, her flower-print blouse billowing over skinny shoulders. My dad sat next to her, his body equally stiff. A bluish haze engulfed everything. Figuring it was a dream, I pinched my forearm.

Nothing changed.

I glanced back at the TV, and Dan Rather was still frozen. I leaned forward and gently poked my mother's shoulder. My finger tingled, as if from a static shock, and slid off. A shadow fluttered by, and I straightened up. A sort of repetitive tribal drumming started in my head. A noise—no, not so much a noise, more like a vibration—hit me, and something dark flittered by in the corner of my vision. Whatever it was seemed to be coming from the hall I had just left. A trickle of sweat rolled down my temple. Something gnawed at my nerves, and I struggled hard not to run. The hall grew darker, a shadow creeping forward at the corners, and I heard a low moan.

That was it.

I darted around the couch and toward the sliding glass door. Tugging at the handle, it refused to move. Then I heard the moan again, sounding even more eerie and tortured than before. I glanced down and realized the door was locked. Pushing up the lever, I bounded outside.

Within moments I had cleared the concrete patio, the grassy lawn, and was fumbling with the latch of the wooden fence. I glanced at the open back door. It seemed miles away now, the morning sunlight gleaming on the glass. I threw back the lever, pulled open the wooden door, and fled out onto the asphalt bike path. Up the trail, I emerged on the sidewalk, the wood-paneled dwellings of my suburban neighborhood swirling in around me. As I peered left and right for oncoming cars, something caught my eye.

Frozen in midair, his head half smashed into a windshield, was a kid. His arms were splayed, his skate deck frozen in midair. One shoe remained, the other suspended in mid-flight.

I knew that kid! It was my brother's friend! Dave something.

I sprinted to the side of the truck and tried stepping up into the wheel well, but some charge pushed me off. I clawed vigorously at the hood but couldn't grip it either. It was then I noticed the sky was darkening.

Clouds were rolling across the sun and a strange mist was rushing in. A shallow breeze bit into my exposed arms and I heard that low moan again. I ran.

Hopping onto the sidewalk, skirting the neighbor's sloppily parked BMW, I stole a glance through their darkened windows. But there was nothing.

I rounded a corner and headed up the street, delving further into the neighborhood. My friend Tim's house was this way, and I debated going there.

What if his place was the same? That thing that seemed to be pursuing me would have me cornered. Was everywhere the same?

I didn't slow down, but hysteria clouded my thinking. I knew Tim had a gun hidden in his house somewhere. He had gone "car hopping", fishing through unlocked vehicles for CDs and valuables. In someone's car, probably that of a peace officer, he had found a huge revolver. I didn't know where he kept it, but I couldn't think of anything else.

The road leading into his court opened and I bounced off the curb and down toward his house. As the road descended, I slowed, a newfound nervousness enveloping me. I glanced back up the hill. Closely shorn lawns fronted wood-paneled houses. The roiling cloud cover broke over, bathing them in a brilliant gleam. Too brilliant.

Was I dreaming?

Hitting the driveway for Tim's house, I rounded the car and scooted into the darkness of the carport. Glancing back up the hill, Tim's dad's boat was in the way. Covered by a tarp, it had not moved in all the time I'd known Tim. I pulled open the screen and pounded on the door.

Nothing.

I squinted through the small window. No sign of life.

Maybe they were just like my parents?

I decided to break in. It wasn't much of a plan, but it was all I could think of. I tried the door, and to my surprise it opened easily.

Darkness greeted me inside. A small table fronted a counter, but it was so dark that I could make out nothing else. I flipped the light switch, but nothing happened. I knew that the hallway on the left led to Tim's room. I headed for it.

I passed the couch that I had spent many a night drinking on, avoiding my parents back home. It was dark and empty now. I glanced up the staircase beside it. It looked hella creepy, and I debated for a moment whether I wanted to enter.

What if that thing, whatever it was, was up there?

I heard a shuffling sound, and I froze.

Wait... Maybe it was Tim? The sound I'd heard before was different. More ephemeral.

Something seemed to be emerging from the shadows near the stairwell, and I stumbled backwards.

"Hello, Aaron."

A polished black shoe emerged from the shadows.

It was the man from downtown! The guy with the fedora!

"What...what are you doing here?"

"Ah, that... that is for another time. You aren't really supposed to be here. You don't know the rules yet, and you are in danger."

"What? I don't understand."

"Not now, later. Follow me."

His sudden presence didn't help matters, but at least he seemed less terrifying than whatever was following me. I ascended the stairs, hesitating slightly as he disappeared around the bend. As I rounded the corner, I saw that the door to Tim's room was open, a gleam of light seeping out.

Tim was in there, hand outstretched, holding aloft a large bag of weed. A tall, figure, long hair flowing over his bearded face, stood in front. His right hand was raised as well, but his oversized sweatshirt obscured all detail. I almost called out to him, but instead glanced over at the man I was following.

"He can't hear you, Aaron."

He opened the closet door and beckoned me toward it. I had seen it before. It was a shallow alcove with just shelves of towels and blankets. Yet as I approached, it was now a black void. I felt a sharp thump on my back, and suddenly I was tumbling in. I screamed, but nothing came out. I tried to thrash my hands and legs, but they felt sluggish and resisted moving. I started to panic. There was a flash, and the next thing I knew I was jerking upright in my bed.

Drenched in sweat, gasping for breath, my Black Flagg t-shirt was plastered to my chest, my shorts tight and sweaty. There was a knock on the door, and before I could do or say anything, my mother had cracked it open. With a look of disapproval, she announced:

"The police are here to see you."

CIVILIZED AUTHORITY

I waved my mother away and sat up groggily. Rising to my feet, I grabbed my leather jacket and fumbled through the inner pocket looking for cigarettes and some matches. Grasping both, I dropped my jacket and ventured out. The den was empty, and I plodded up the stairs, resignation mixing with a touch of apprehension. I'd had plenty of run-ins with the local police. Most involved trumped-up charges manufactured to harass "my kind."

In what came as no great surprise, both my parents were at the kitchen table finishing breakfast. Their stern looks a sharp reproach in the light of early morning. Par for the course.

"Aaron..."

"Yes, Dad. I know."

I spat it out, annoyed at the disgust in his voice. The door was open, a couple of uniformed police officers just beyond. The most forward one was a bit overweight, his round face not completely unfriendly. He looked young, not quite the jock douchebag of most of the cops.

"Are you Aaron Law?"

I lit my cigarette, shaking out and tossing the match. The early morning sunlight was overpowering. It made my head hurt and forced me to squint. The shade of the carport was the only thing that made it bearable, the white concrete of the driveway just beyond an almost unviewable blaze.

"Yeah."

"We need you to come downtown."

"Am I in trouble?"

"We'll talk about it downtown."

"Can I finish my cigarette first?"

"I'll open the rear window. You can smoke in the car."

That was a first. I nodded and followed them out into the blazing sunlight. As I slid onto the slick black leather seat the window rolled down automatically. I was used to what I guess you would call "central booking." The officer stationed there was always pretending he was busy doing paperwork. Fingerprints at the counter and mugshots in a separate room would follow, administered by gruff officers who regarded me with disdain.

This time it was different. They led me in through a nondescript door at the rear and took me into a small, plain room of whitewashed brick. In the center was a heavy-duty table. I entered and took a seat. The officer escorting me closed the door behind. I looked up and noticed a video camera hugging the corner of the ceiling. This felt like a cell. I breathed out deeply and slumped over the table.

Minutes ticked by. I had no sense of how long I sat there. There was no clock on the walls, and I didn't have my watch. After what seemed like an hour the lock flipped loudly and two men in black suits came in. One slightly thicker than the other, his pale face garnished with faint traces of salt and pepper stubble. The other looked no less intimidating for his slightly smaller size, only a bit more rodent-like. They sat down across from me.

"So, Aaron, we have a specialty here, don't we?"

It was the smaller one, and his bluntness caught me off guard.

"I... I..."

"Take your time. Just keep in mind we will recognize when you lie to us."

"I'm not, I mean, I'm nothing special..."

"Oh, you are very special, Aaron. Even a little dangerous."

"We've been following you. There are plenty of people who will want to use and abuse you. Maybe even kill you. We can prevent that."

I didn't trust them. My encounters with controlled authority had already been filled with lies and misdirection, and these two had the feel of something even worse. I'd had enough of being talked down to by my dad to directly call them out, but I felt the need to get out as soon as possible.

"I'm just... just a kid! Skateboarding! Rock and Roll! That sort of thing. I don't know what you're talking about..."

I felt a flush coming over my face. I had read plenty of horror stories and been privy to quite a few conspiracy theories. They could lock me up. Hide me from civilized society. Make me disappear. No one except my friends cared anything about me, and they were considered to be funny looking, rebellious kids. What could they do? My dad would probably just agree with whatever the police told him. He might even help them out.

"There is no use playing stupid with us, Aaron."

There was something about their expressions, their stares seemed cold and calculated. The only hope I had—and it was a slim one—was if I could convince them I was just a normal, fucked up kid.

"Look, Aaron. Tell you what. We'll give you a week to think about this."

Almost in unison, they got up and walked out. Just as the heftier one was closing the door, he turned around.

"We know about New York. And DC. Don't make the wrong decision."

A cold wave washed over me. I sat stock still, trying desperately not to show any emotion as he turned and exited.

I let a minute or two pass before I stood up and approached the door. The knob turned, and it opened it. I pried the door wider and peered out, half expecting them to be still there. But the hallway was empty. Just tiled floors and dim fluorescent lighting.

The walkway ended with a sharp turn, and I rounded it only to come face to face with a thickly painted white door. The top was crested with a small window of semi-opaque glass, and there were silhouettes moving beyond. I pressed my ear to the glass and listened.

Just muted dialogue.

Opening the door, I faced the backs of a huddle of uniformed police officers. One turned.

"Hey, what are you doing here?"

"I was in the exam room."

"How'd you get there?"

"You guys took me in."

"What guys?"

He was clearly annoyed, his face wrinkled in disgust. He obviously didn't approve of my punk rock appearance or Black Flagg "Police Story" t-shirt.

"I... I don't know his name..."

"You're trespassing, kid. We could lock you up for that. From the looks of you, might do you some good. Help make you not be such a faggot."

I burned at the insult, but I had learned the hard way that giving cops lip doesn't pay. I glanced over at the video screen topping the desk.

"Take a look, it's all recorded."

The officer scowled.

"What room were you in?"

"I don't know the room number, but if you look..."

Just then, another officer came around the corner.

"That's him! That's the guy that brought me here!"

It was a dead ringer for the same guy, only now in a police uniform. The officer looked put off. Glancing at me in disgust, he casually remarked-

"I've never seen this kid before. So, Don, what say we grab some lunch."

"But I..."

"Get the fuck out of here, kid. Before I change my mind and lock you up."

I decided to look at the floor and leave quickly. The back of my head burning with their stares, I walked over to the front door and out into the blinding sunlight. A bleached concrete sidewalk spread out before me, the buildings of downtown Fairfax, Virginia just beyond. I walked steadily toward the edge of the building, trying not to look around. Hitting the corner, I broke into a run. Up the grassy median, across the parking lot of some office building, around square-cut bushes, and onto a tree-sheltered sidewalk. With a quick glance up and down the street, I launched myself across a two-lane highway. I flew past a queue of elegant two-story mansions and at the first cross-street, I took a dip into the adjoining neighborhood. My lungs were on fire, but I didn't dare slow down. Maintaining a frantic pace, trying to stay in the neighborhoods and off the highway, it took me almost an hour to make it home.

Panting and sweating as I came in the front door, I received a quizzical, disappointed look from my mom. Passing her, I headed down the steps and to my room. Plopping down on the bed, my mind was a scatter-shot of images and half-formed plans. I had to get away. Out of this house. Maybe I could get a job. Something closer to downtown that I could ride my bike to. Maybe even a cheap place to live. I could possibly stay with friends, but I might just drag them into this. Most lived with their parents and were in no position to move out. Besides, those guys would track me.

How did they know so much? I ended up in the hospital in New York, so there was probably a public record of that. But DC?

I had a friend in Centreville, less than an hour away. He knew a lot of people. People off the grid in Blacksburg and Richmond. Punk rock group houses and the like. He might be able to help. He was grumpy and weird, and it could be hard getting anything out of him, but maybe the seriousness of the situation would sway him. If he believed a word of it. Even at the best of times he could be hard to convince.

NOTHING IS WHAT IT SEEMS

I changed into jeans, a Misfits "Bullet" T-shirt, combat boots, and slipped on my leather jacket. As I grabbed my skateboard, I popped open the window. It led out into the back yard, and exiting this way might buy me a little time. I didn't necessarily think my parents were in on whatever was going on—they had too much of a herd mentality for that—but they kissed any authority figure's ass, and they would turn me over to the cops in a heartbeat. I edged over the windowsill, down the wall, and crept across the freshly mowed grass. Opening the latch on the gate, I stepped onto the bike trail, flipped my skateboard over, and took off. Down the narrow path, across a tiny bridge, through a small, abandoned parking lot, and out into a neighborhood beyond. I figured I should stick to the back roads, close to houses and woods I could disappear into.

It took about a half-hour, skating through genteel, cardboard cutout developments. Suspicious middle-age douchebags gave me the occasional hard looks. More than once their jock-o-rama offspring tossed an insult as I passed, their attention only momentarily diverted from the sponge bath they were lovingly giving their chromed-out trucks. Playing football, going to church on Sundays, biding time until they died. God, I hated Fairfax.

I rounded Tapestry Drive and headed up Braddock Road. The blinding sun of early 'morn on this road always added bite to my morning hangovers as I stumbled to my shitty minimum wage jobs. Wind whistled through the branches beside me. Leaves the color of rust fluttered past. The air felt charged, the edges of everything slightly blurred. Although it might have been my imagination. I felt like I was nursing a hangover.

The wind was cold, and it was autumn, but my skin kept flushing hot. Burke Station Road emerged, and I waited for a couple of cars to pass before crossing over. Ollieing up the curb, the overhanging trees closed in like a matchstick tunnel and threw bands of shade across the narrow roadway. A headache set in just as the wheels of my skateboard caught a stick, and almost toppled me over. Losing the board, I righted myself and shook my head, trying to clear cobwebs that never seemed to leave now.

I felt a strange pull to the right and naively headed that way. After only a slight buffer of high grass I stumbled through a small, wooded enclave and into a meadow littered with gravestones. I had never paid this place much attention. A small memorial cemetery that I assumed held nothing special. The grass was tall and unkempt, much heartier than the half-dead yellowing clumps I recalled. The gravestones looked different as well. Larger and more arcane, their facades heavily worn yet still ornate. Moss and lichen were making steady headway, slowly reconquering the crumbling blocks. I remembered them being milquetoast modern tombstones, but these looked ancient. I didn't recall that at all. In fact, I couldn't recall the last time I'd seen moss growing on anything in Virginia. Then it struck me. None of the tombstones displayed any aspect of Christianity. No crosses, saints, or angels. I had been to plenty of cemeteries, including the one in Sleepy Hollow, and even the oldest gravestones there displayed something Christian.

The writing was mostly worn away, but what little remained didn't even look English. My toes felt cold and damp, and I glanced down. A sheen of dew covered everything, beading in small drops across the toe caps of my boots. The wind had picked up, a winter sharpness augmenting its bite. A heavy shadow rolled across the grass, and I looked up. The sky was now a roiling mass of thunderclouds. Angry storm heads churning against one another in a turbulent battlefield that spanned the heavens. This was looking like rain, and I peered towards the far side of the cemetery. I thought I recalled a small congregation of trees there.

What skirted the edges was far darker and more overgrown than I recalled. Rain broke out. Big, fat drops that splashed cold as ice against my face. I headed for the trees, navigating through a maze of crumbling gravestones and waist-high grass. The smell of wet earth gave way to the fragrant scent of pine. The ground before me spread out in a series of small hills and troughs, an unending blanket of needles coating the last vestiges of boulders and small plants. I noticed it wasn't raining here. Despite the dense canopy there should be some rain coming through. I turned back around to see if the rain had stopped but the cemetery was nowhere to be found.

My skin grew cold. I had no idea what to do and everything looked the same, Going forward seemed as good a bet as any.

A WORLD AFIRE

It seemed like hours since I had entered the woods, yet there was no end in sight. The landscape had grown brighter, filtered sunlight now descending from the overhead branches. I would pass thickets of vine that dangled like a leviathan from the trees. Giant mushrooms, puffed up in giant balls, dotted the terrain. Small, straggly bushes started to pop up and the trees were changing as well. Pine giving way to birch and oak. I passed a small meadow, the golden tips of its weeds tossing about in the wind. Then I heard a muffled mechanical screech. Scooping up the board, I darted for a nearby large oak. The cry erupted again, only much louder this time. It sounded like a man's voice, and I recalled the men in the police station.

Had they followed me? What if they installed a tracking device? That would explain DC! But when could they have implanted it? All the way back in New York? In the hospital? But how would they have known? That man, downtown, he would have had a chance, but I don't get the feeling he's one of them.

A bustle of activity interrupted my reverie. A manic scurrying, followed by heavy breathing.

Suddenly, a girl flew by. Young and attractive, her long brunette hair was matted and frayed, strings of it clinging to the sweat on her face. She was barefoot, cuts and scrapes visible under smears of grime. She kept ducking down, peering desperately over her shoulder. A loud burst of gunfire erupted, and she flew forward, geysers of blood erupting from her chest. My mouth fell open, and I tucked myself back behind the nearest oak. As her prone body flopped down, there was another squawk, in what sounded like a foreign tongue. I crouched, concealing myself as well as possible. A man came into view, his outfit similar to the British World War I fatigues I'd seen in history books. His face was hidden behind a black gas mask, and he held a rifle aloft. He trotted up to the dead girl and gave her a probing stab. Her face mostly buried in a tangled mass of hair, one of her small breasts popped out, it's puffy areola looking somehow obscene with its lifeless exposure. Her body moved limply with the jabs and the soldier turned his head, gave a short nod, and stepped aside. Another stepped into view, bearing the twin tanks of a flame thrower on his back. Positioning the nozzle over the dead girl, a torrent of flame shot out. Two more times it erupted, reducing the body to blackened gristle and seared bone.

I felt like throwing up, but was too terrified to risk even that, my throat buckling as I dry heaved. The voices squawked again, the man with the rifle looking about. Then, they both turned and walked away, leaving the smoldering carcass behind.

The last licks of flame died out, some of the bones still aglow. Time passed. Maybe half an hour, maybe only ten minutes, but I couldn't hold it any longer. I crept around the trunk, peeking in the direction from which the men had come. There was no trace of them. I snatched up my board and bolted, the needles crunching far too loudly underfoot as I fled.

The uneven terrain, my leather jacket, and the heaviness of my boots slowed me down, but I was terrified, and kept my eyes forward. My heart beat madly in my chest, trickles of sweat rolled down my forehead, and I panted wildly. Roots underfoot clutched at me, throwing me off and threatening a spill, but I managed to stay upright. The edge of the woods came into view, and I sped up. My legs were on fire now, my arm aching under the weight of the board, but I was almost out!

The last of the trees fell away, as I burst out into sunlight. I was in a recently shorn meadow. The sudden overflow of light was momentarily blinding, but I could make out the forms of buildings just beyond. Relief washed over. At the end of the field was the small road of a development. I slowed, blinking my eyes, my breath ragged gasps.

As my eyes grew more accustomed, I noticed blackened mounds on my periphery. I turned to examine the closest one, and almost cried out. It was the skeleton of a human, crumpled woefully and reminding me of the girl in the woods. The bones were roasted clean, the ground around them blackened and just showing signs of new growth. Not far off, three similar clumps marred the grassy plot. I could see what looked like the traces of more blackened remnants strewn across the road and for the first time I got a good look at the buildings.

Opulent, multi-storied houses, with most of the upper window frames seared and blackened. Some of the lower ones were boarded up, tendrils of soot still peeping out. Then I realized that all the lower windows and the doors were barricaded from the outside!

I ventured out onto the street and slowly wandered across. None of these buildings looked anything like Fairfax. Short barriers of stone topped by a queue of iron spikes walled them in.

This might be worse than the woods! I was out in the open here, I had no idea where I was, and whoever those people were, they didn't appear to be friendly.

I dropped my board and started down the street, gaining momentum as I flew by buildings that eventually dwindled into single-story houses. Many sported flowing, if overgrown, green lawns. A few were cloistered behind chain link fences, and only a few of these houses were boarded up. All sported the gaping holes of what were once windows, the interiors a blackened maw. I was so busy taking it all in I almost slammed into the front of a car. Stopping short at the last moment, I stopped and stared.

The wiry frame of what had once been a sedan, now reduced to a charred skeletal corpse, lay in the middle of the road. The wheels were partially melted, the windows long gone.

I considered returning to the woods. They had led me into this nightmare, and they were the only possibility I could think of to get out. The wind was dying down. Dark clouds were rolling overhead, their underbellies a radiant orange. The shadows of the buildings grew longer and evening was approaching. The last thing I wanted was to be lost in those woods at night.

Then again, out in the open like this might not be much better.

Then I heard something that sounded like human voices. I couldn't make out any words, but they sounded half-frenzied. I hopped on my skateboard and headed toward the noise.

I skated around more burnt-out cars as I homed in on the sound. It grew louder and the street opened into two lanes, the sprawling grounds of what looked like a school just beyond. The noise was coming from that direction, and it sounded like hundreds of people. Some talking, some yelling, some wailing, but none of it in English. The dialect sounded Asian, but I couldn't place the accent. I wondered how I should approach. This was probably a stupid move on my part. I should be running the opposite way, toward the woods. But I was curious and not sure what to do. I sidled over to the curb and stepped into the shelter of a tree line. Staying in the shade, hiding amongst the giant trunks, I slunk forward.

I could make out a large, boxed white sign just ahead. Huge Asian characters were imprinted on it, with a smaller line of English letters beneath that stated, "Woodside High School." It fronted a giant chain-link fence, crested with razor wire. Dirt-smeared fingers grasped the links, the malnourished bodies of at least a hundred people thronging about. Some were covered in large, pus-filled boils. Blood and grime seemed to compete for exposed skin on most of the mob. Their cheeks were sunken, their skeletal limbs clashing against one another in a frenzy of horror. The wailing intensified. A younger man with a face that would be handsome if it weren't covered by sores, started scaling the fence. His hands flew over each other in a flurry, his bloody bare toes wrapping themselves around each lower link. He almost made it to the razor wire when a voice sounded over a microphone. He continued undeterred, furiously struggling toward the top. He had just made it, his fingers wrapping around the top pole, when the bark of a large caliber gun sounded. Bloody chunks flew from his chest, and he slumped into the razor wire. The frantic cries of the crowd swelled, and a few more started scaling the fence. Rapid bursts of gunfire ticked off in a cacophony of flying metal and torn flesh. I followed the line of sight of the bursts and spotted a watchtower. Drifting out was a trail of smoke from what looked like a mounted fifty caliber. Over the roar of the crowd, I started to hear a dull thumping noise. It grew steadily louder until a black dot appeared on the horizon; a black dot that was slowly transforming into something else. This was getting far too sketchy. I turned and ran, hugging the tree line as I fled. Bursting back onto the side street, I mounted my skateboard and took off. Weaving in and out of the remnants of cars and corpses, I tried to keep low, hoping I was fast enough.

I had just reached what I assumed was downtown when the overhead thumping suddenly grew much louder. I glanced over my shoulder and saw the silhouette of a helicopter cresting the far house. I sped up, skating as fast as I could. A loud voice crackled in the air, shouting gibberish in a language I didn't understand, and a minute later, the pavement flared up in a burst of gunfire. Stone shrapnel pelted me as I pounded my feet against pavement as hard as I could. A burst exploded just in front, the eruption jolting me from my board. I tumbled over, crying out as my knee scraped along the asphalt, taking a chunk of my skin with it. Scrambling to my feet, I scooped up my board, bounded the curb, and headed toward the woods. Tufts of grass erupted under the airborne assault as I tried to dodge and weave.

"Fuck! Fuck! Fuck!"

Suddenly my board shot out of my hand, a wheel tearing off under the impact. A blind terror seized me, and I half-dashed, half-dove for the woods. Chunks of bark pelted me as I landed heavily on my shoulder, the surrounding trunks flying apart under a hail of bullets. Springing back up, I scrambled into the cover of the trees.

More unintelligible squawking, and then everything turned into a flurry of airborne vegetation. The bass-heavy thump of a Gatling gun and the roar of woods disintegrating under the assault. I tucked in my head and ran, gasping for air and regretting every cigarette I had ever smoked. Bullets tore by, some mere inches away. A flood of adrenaline pushed me forward, surging back in force with each narrow miss.

Eventually the torrent of fire faded. Sharp cracks still resounded occasionally, but the barrage was lessening.

Sweat rolled down my temples and my legs were shot. I slowed and looked around. I had no idea where I was.

THE REMAINS

After what seemed an eternity, the woods started to thin. I had left in the early morning, and now it should have been late evening, but under the shelter of the trees it had never actually grown dark. Now it was growing light again and stranger still, the light had that bluish-yellow tint of late morning. It had been an interminably long day, but not so long that I might have skipped a night.

The trees thinned out as the terrain flowed across a sprawling carpet of waist-deep grass. A couple of contorted trees were interspersed on the sprawling savannah, their autumn-hued leaves twisting in the wind. I stumbled out, blinking and trying to peer beyond the immediate horizon. Looking for a hill, a development, anything, but everything in the distance was obscured by a hazy mist. As I wandered farther, the uneven firmament pitched me forward a few times. The stiff soles of my combat boots didn't help. It was warm, and under my leather jacket I was starting to feel uncomfortable.

After about twenty minutes I had made it past the first of the scattered trees and could see something in the distance. It was still unclear in the mist, but I could make out a few dark edges. I slowed and was starting to collect my breath when I noticed something nearby in a clump of tall weeds. I wasn't sure until I was right up on it, but it turned out to be a tennis shoe. The edges were scuffed and stained, and most of the white had degraded into a cream color. I kicked it and it scuttled forward, a slight crust of dirt breaking apart in a powdery spurt. The shoe must have been there quite a while. But if there's a sneaker, there is probably something resembling civilization nearby.

As I continued through the meadow, I saw something farther afield. I slowed as I approached, the mass slowly materializing into legs and a torso. Swaddled by dark jeans, one foot was missing a shoe. The other was outfitted by the same kind I had come across. Goosebumps sprouted on my neck and arms.

This didn't look good.

Scanning around for something to prod this thing with, I circled the body and could see that the front portion was buried in a nest of grass. I nudged the body with my foot. It didn't budge. I pushed a little harder but lost my balance and almost fell over, swaying unsteadily for a moment.

I inched forward, nestled the tip of my boot under the curve of the ribcage, and tried to heft it up. It still didn't budge. A trickle of sweat rolled down my face, the tips of my hair falling into my eyes. I scooped my hair back, edged forward a little more, and put my back into the effort. With a disgusting squelch, it broke free and rolled over.

It didn't have a head! And half the chest was gone!

A gash flowed down from the neck in almost clinical precision, Fragments of concisely cut bone jutted out from a dark red sheath of flesh. That was enough to make me hurl, what little was in my stomach fighting to come up. Then something squirmed and I saw the maggots. I lost it, stumbling backward as I puked a trail of foamy liquid.

I was doubled over, coughing, and spitting up phlegm when I heard a whistle. In a panic, I straightened and rose to my feet. It appeared to be coming from the forward line of trees, the glare of the sunlight obscuring the details, but I thought I could make out a person. Cupping my hand over my brow, I could see someone waving. Then it occurred to me that the hands weren't waving, they seemed to be indicating...

That I should get down?

The overhead noise was growing louder, and I dropped. Sprawling in the weeds, I cursed myself for leaving the woods. Turning my head as inconspicuously as possible, I rotated my eyes all the way to the corners of their sockets. At first, I saw only the blue sky. Then the air seemed to ripple, and I tried to will my body deeper into the ground.

Then I saw it.

A silvery gleam that was mostly disc like, reflecting the sun in a blaze of glory. The blades of grass around me started whipping in convulsions.

After a few moments, the sound receded. I waited a moment longer, ears peeled, and then scrambled to my feet, running in the direction of the trees. The wooded line bobbed up and down as I darted through the weeds. I almost tripped every few feet, but kept my eyes trained on the spot I had seen someone.

I was rewarded at the tree line when a head popped out from behind a trunk. It looked like a teenage girl, her nappy dreds falling all about her tan face. She edged out a little further, her small breasts and puffy nipples pushing against a white tank top. I stumbled forward, falling into the shade of the trees. I was just righting myself when I felt a tug. She had grabbed my wrist and was pulling me aloft. Her eyes darting around frantically, she dragged me in.

We passed through a thin grove and into the enclave of what looked like a suburb from hell. Pitted and mutilated black tar streets, fallen branches and rocky debris strewn across. Tall townhouses surrounded us, their windows ribbed with shards of broken glass. The short front yards were encircled by chain link fences, and half of the front doors were missing. Many of the lower windows were boarded up. On some, the second story walls had broken down, the gashes providing a view of rotted floorboards and cobweb-shrouded furniture. There were traces of crumpled blankets and sleeping bags amidst the clutter, as if the abandoned tenements had harbored squatters at some point.

All the lawns were overgrown with clusters of weeds and detritus, some of it organic, some human. A few of the houses sported the occasional automobile, their windows smashed out and a few missing whole chucks. It had obviously happened a while ago, the raw edges blistering with rust. The girl let go of my hand and, gesturing for me to follow, headed up a driveway. She passed the corpse of a blue Toyota and dashed into an overgrown path beside. I followed, my head tucked slightly, my eyes darting about as I tried to determine where we could possibly be. This looked like the abandoned remnants of a neighborhood. I had seen houses like this in the more ghetto sections of DC. But there they were nestled next to functional townhouses. This whole neighborhood looked like it had been abandoned years ago.

I swerved around overgrown purple feelers as she rounded a whitewashed half wall and dropped out of view. Closing in a moment later she was gone. A short staircase of soiled steps led to a closed door, a musty smell emanating from the depths.

This was growing sketchy.

There was a hiss, followed by another, and then her arms re-emerged, gesturing frantically for me to come down. I held still, thinking for all the world that this looked like a setup. Her head came back into view, her face desperately pleading. I decided staying put was probably at least as dangerous as following her and headed down the steps.

As I entered, I wrinkled my nose and blinked my eyes, trying to adjust to the sudden darkness. A scraping sound greeted me, and I started to back away, cursing myself for entering. Then, the girl's face popped up. Gesturing for me to follow as she returned to a small fire. She was blowing on it, fanning the flames with her hands. She fed it a few sticks, saving one to stir the glowing pile. After a few minutes she stopped, stood up, and headed for the now visible corner. In the light of the flames, I could see a blackened concrete wall. The smoke was already aggravating my eyes but I could make out the dust-covered hulks of what looked like a washer and a pile of stained blankets. There was a door just beyond. Consisting of just a few planks and a simple black latch, two by fours were nailed across it. I glanced back at the girl, and she'd produced a few cans and a small, blackened frying pan. Crouched in a half-squat, she stabbed the edge of one of the cans with what looked like a large Bowie knife, peeling the top off in one deft swoop. She put the knife down, wrapped her hand in a stained towel, picked up the frying pan, and dumped the contents in. It looked like some sort of meat hash. Passing it gently over the fire, the contents started to throb and fizzle. Pulling out two plates, she scraped the hash onto them. Setting the pan next to the now dying fire, she scurried over to a pile of clothing in the corner.

A moment later she returned with two forks. Squatting back down and digging them into the meaty piles, she raised up a plate and offered it to me. I was blinking incessantly, the thick smog making my eyes burn, but I reached forward as gracefully as I could manage and accepted. Grabbing the fork, I twirled the tip through the quickly hardening pile. I glanced over, and she was devouring hers. Wanting not to appear rude, I picked up a small portion and raised it to my lips, blew on it, then swallowed. Meaty hash, just like I thought. I hadn't realized how hungry I was, and the food tasted surprisingly good. The girl finished her portion, stood up, and wandered over to the corner. She scooped up a dishrag and started to wipe her plate clean. It made me wonder if either plate had ever been washed. But I decided that under the circumstances it didn't really matter. It also didn't hurt that she was so cute. Despite her small size she didn't act like a child. I couldn't help but notice the hair under her arms. So, she was past puberty, but that's all I knew. Her tank top and green BDUs didn't exactly look like kid's clothing, and I couldn't help staring at her perfectly round butt as she leaned over. Her back still turned, she dug at something in the pile, her clothes separating at the waist to reveal the crack of her ass. I finished the hash, and just as I was setting the plate down, she turned around and held up a bottle. The glass was dark and green, the bottom half enshrined in a tight weave of rope. She took a swig, wiped her mouth with the back of her hand, and offered me the bottle.

It burned, but it wasn't unpleasant. Some kind of wine, strong but fortified. Way better than the Thunderbird or Wild Irish Rose me and my friends usually managed to get our hands on. The flame had died down to a flicker and I appreciated the small warmth it provided. My eyes were mostly used to the smoke by now, and I wasn't blinking so much. The room had grown darker, the wisps of the dying fire casting a flickering glow on the walls. She squatted down beside me and took the bottle. Throwing back her head, she took another swig. Looking neither at me nor the fire, she handed over the bottle. The wine had gone to my head, and I felt... connected? The whole scenario seemed to be growing more normal. I glanced over at the girl.

Did she quickly look away?

She was staring at the fire, as if lost in thought. I tried not to make it obvious as I edged closer. She didn't move.

Did I stand a chance? Would I ruin it?

She looked back at me, and she wasn't holding up her hand for the bottle.

I never was good at this! Did she want me to kiss her?

Emboldened by the wine, I leaned in. Everything seemed a bit surreal, my eyes were half-closed, and I acted as naturally as I could, trying to ignore the burning tension creeping up the sides of my face. She started to reach for the bottle and paused, her dark eyes boring in. I couldn't make out their meaning.

Was it fear? Anger? A welcome?

Then she smiled slightly, and I dove in. Her mouth opened, and we were kissing. Next thing I knew, we were stripping off each other's clothes. I had only had sex twice before, but I didn't want to come off as an amateur. The first time, I couldn't stop talking. I was a complete idiot. The second time, I had this cocky bravura, like I was a pro. I felt ridiculous afterwards. This time, I just tried to take it naturally. I had this feeling that this wasn't really me, more a projection of who I wanted to be, and that helped tremendously. There was no burden of a normal life to try and live up to. Or live down. I wasn't even sure if she spoke English. Not that it mattered. She pulled me back gently, drawing a blanket from the nearby pile. I reached to take off her tank top, but she was way ahead of me. She had small breasts, with dark, half-dollar areolas, the nipples firmly erect. Her olive skin was soft and smooth. I ran my hands down her sides until I came to the top of her pants, gently pushing them down. She loosed her hands from the relaxed hug she had around my shoulders and pushed them off. She was now naked, and I still had most of my clothes on. I bent over and fought with the laces of my boots, her hands interrupting my progress as she pushed off my jacket and lifted my shirt. I had freed one foot, and was working on the second, when I felt her hands grasping at my belt buckle. She had it unfastened and was tugging down my pants just as I managed to kick the second boot off. Standing naked before her I felt cold and a bit shy.

Slowly and evenly, we enjoyed each other's bodies. It was the best feeling I had ever known. Afterwards we lay coiled around each other, the last embers of the fire dying as I reached over and pulled a second blanket over top. Then we did it again.

A LITTLE CASE OF OCD

I woke up to a dusty gloom. Sitting bolt upright, and I pulled the blanket over my skinny, naked chest. Pushing the hair out of my eyes, I could see that she was fully clothed. Sidled up next to the fire, she was looking at me with a steady gaze. Her eyes connected with mine, and the corners of her mouth twitched in a smile. It was enough to break the tension. I smiled back, and immediately felt self-conscious. My ears burned, my face flushed, and I looked around anxiously for my clothes.

Grabbing at my underwear, shirt, and pants, I pulled them over and dressed. I felt out of sorts, but when I glanced up the girl was staring at the door. I looked around, taking in the dusty, bare basement.

It was just a concrete floor, with cement blocks for walls. A single window marked the far corner, a crude barricade of timber blocking most of its light. Dusty moats saturated the air, and I noticed that the basement looked even more dilapidated in the light of day.

I heard a distant yell. Tying my boots, I grappled desperately for my jacket. She was on her feet already, backing toward the far wall as she kept her eyes glued to the door. In her hand she held aloft that same Bowie knife from last night.

The sound grew louder. She scuttled alongside the door frame, her right hand holding the blade above her head. The doorknob rattled, followed by a loud pounding, the steel frame vibrating with every blow.

"You bitch! Open the door! I know you're in there!"

It was the voice of a man, and he spoke English! Did that mean the girl spoke English too?

The pounding resounded again; the blows augmented by the sound of kicks. The ear-piercing crack of a submachine gun rang out. More gunfire, and the door erupted, the handle flying off in a burst of silvery debris. With a sharp kick, the door flew open, and in strode a stocky man, his sunburnt face sporting a five o'clock shadow. Outfitted in charcoal BDUs, and he held aloft an SKS.

"I know you're in here, you fucking bitch!"

Just as he said it and stepped through the doorframe, her hand sliced upward. The blade slashed across his wrist, and he screamed as his arm erupted in a geyser of blood, the gun clattering loudly to the floor. She gave him a swift kick and he buckled, slamming into the wall. Sliding down, his left hand gripped his wrist tightly as blood streamed around his fingers.

"Fuck you, you little fucking bitch! I'll kill you!"

He glanced up, muttered-

"Oh, fuck,"

and scrambled up the steps and out of sight. The girl looked over and waved for me to approach. I shuffled over, as she slipped up the steps. The sidewall was almost shoulder high, the bushes topping it providing additional cover, but I still tried to keep my head lower than the concrete.

She stopped at the apex, glanced around, and motioned for me to follow. I scrambled up, just hitting the top step as she took off. Rounding the corner, she made it into the shadow of a nearby bush. She was signaling intently, and I darted for her.

I was almost there when I heard an intense crack and dove into the grass. Light flashed nearby; the burst so intense that brilliance streamed through the cracks in my sheltering arms. The girl hissed and scampered out to get me. Grabbing my wrists, she pulled into the barbed leaves. She held a finger up to her lips, drew out the knife, and glanced around the edge. Motioning for me to follow, she swallowed a deep breath and sprinted out of the shade. As I trailed close on her heels, we crossed the lawn, hurdled a curb, and careened into a pockmarked street. She was moving quickly, and I struggled to keep up. Bounding over potholes, my feet caught on raised clefts of concrete a few times, almost throwing me forward. Combat boots are not made for running, and my leather jacket felt stifling. I was breathing through my mouth, my heart pounding in my chest, the bright sun forcing me to squint. She crossed a small road and hopped onto the opposite sidewalk. Gasping for air, my legs starting to ache, I swiveled my head toward the wall of chain-link fronted lawns. That was when I noticed the bodies.

They didn't even look real. Completely bleached out skeletons, bent and contorted as if in the throes of agony. They had obviously been there quite a while, some of the weeds twisting up through labyrinths of bone. I slowed, staring at one.

"You slow, you be like them."

I was startled and turned to her.

"What... what happened here?"

Her expression didn't change. I wasn't even sure if she even understood.

"This..."

I pointed to the crumpled skeleton.

"Who did this?"

Her gaze broke, and she looked around nervously. Then she waved for me to follow.

"No! This? What is this?"

She waved more intensely, her other hand pointing skyward. In a low voice she muttered-

"They. They come back."

"What? Who is they?"

She looked truly afraid now. Head slightly lowered as she motioned vigorously for me.

"Quickly!"

She bit her bottom lip and started running again, glancing back to make sure I was right behind. Around another corner, and the houses fell away, rows of trees closing in on all sides. They harbored only a few leaves, the last stragglers dying a fiery yellow and orange death. The girl was moving fast, the distance between us increasing, and I picked up pace to try and catch up. The woods were falling away into patchy fields of tall weeds and muddy watering holes. The road was disintegrating as well, morphing into a dirt trail. Just ahead, the outlines hazy in the cloudy light, was a huge, boxy structure. It looked like a massive industrial warehouse. Soiled brick walls whose upper echelons were punctuated by tightly latticed windows. The air had started to smell of scorched metal and industrial chemicals. The trail broke out into an asphalt parking lot. As the building came into view, I noticed two closed garage bays. Their doors looked old and worn, their elevated platforms harboring a slit for what must have been a retractable ramp. She rounded one and scurried up a stairway. Reaching the side door, she slowed and knocked softly.

She was still standing there, ear tilted toward the door, when I caught up. Gasping, my hands on my knees, she rapped again, harder this time. A minute or two passed, and I had caught enough of my breath to straighten up.

With an impatient look, she twisted the metal knob. Glancing at me, holding a finger to her lips, she eased in.

The interior was dark and accompanied by the smell of an old basement. I could make out the forms of immense metal pipes, their hulking silhouettes hiding anything beyond. She motioned for me with her free arm. I glanced behind and followed.

THE PROBLEM WITH TIGHT SPACES

I closed the door instinctively, the enveloping darkness hiding all but shimmering outlines. She pressed up against the wall, knife at the ready. Ahead I could make out the glimmering edges of something silver and immense. Without turning her head, she waved me forward and darted into the shadowed room. I followed, the darkness swallowing me up. A moment of panic flashed through, as I thought I'd lost her, but then a small hand reached out and grabbed me. Moving slowly, one foot in front of the other, I wasn't sure where we were headed. Just as I started to inch forward, a hand pushed into my stomach, and I almost lost my balance. The edges of something gleamed in front. Squinting harder, I could make out the dark forms of steel beams spider-webbing across the ceiling. My eyes followed the glint over the curve of a hulking object in front, but all I could see was the silhouette of something immense.

Out of nowhere my head started to pound, and I fell to my knees gasping for air. There was a wet, slurping sound, and double pinpricks gleamed in the shadows. As they drew closer, a row of sharp teeth trailing a steam of drool emerged. The pounding increased, the hissing grew louder, and I doubled over. A flash, a piercing scream, and pain dug into the back of my skull.

My eyes clenched shut, and when I managed to open them, hot and salty tears trickled in. I wiped at them madly, glancing down through stinging vision at the shadowed forms of my arms. Something dark and viscous had splattered across my sleeves, and I could feel drops of it clinging to my face. A hand pulled me to my feet. My vision was clearing through repeated blinks, and I thought I could see a blade dripping a dark, thick fluid. I stumbled backwards and saw that a dwarfish gray form lay curled at my feet, dark fluid trickling from its neck. Something pushed me, bringing me back to reality, and I turned. Her back to me, the girl was waving for me to leave. I retreated a few feet, when she swiveled her head and hissed-

"Run!"

Stumbling back, I turned, and did just that.

It was so dark I could barely see. I passed what was apparently the T-section we had come out of and kept going. Glancing behind me I couldn't see the girl.

Should I go back? She'd pushed me forward for a reason. Whatever this was, she knew far more than I. Maybe she had a plan and was circling around to see me?

I felt like a coward. But what could I do? If she had engineered my escape, and I went right back in, it would all be in vain.

Right?

The rationalizing didn't help. Maybe it was sublimated machismo, but I couldn't just leave her. I slowed, moved closer to the wall, and started back.

Minutes passed.

Where was that T-section we came through?

More time passed as I walked, eventually totaling what must have been an hour. A feeling of dread washed over, and panic started to creep in.

Was I lost?

I felt the hot burning of oncoming exasperation, my eyes watering in frustration. I slowed my pace, looking around. Then I noticed that the pathway was growing brighter, and I could make out that the walls were lined with a network of enormous pipes. I looked down and saw that my boots were scraping across a metal grate. The air was cool and felt thick, like it was damp.

Had it always been that way? I seemed to recall it being mustier, but now it had the distinctive smell of brine.

A dim light emanating from I knew not where had kicked in so gradually I had barely noticed it. Looking up, a complex lattice of beams crisscrossed one another overhead, their pattern so intricate that I couldn't make out a ceiling beyond.

Where the fuck was I?

What must have been another hour passed, the dim illumination continuing virtually unchanged. Eventually an opening harboring a gently sloping ramp emerged. It swooped up towards a large steel door that was circled by what looked like raised metal rib bones. A thick glass porthole earmarked the center, a small wheel just below.

Stepping up, I gripped the wheel and turned. It moved slightly and then froze. Throwing all my weight against it and pushing, the wheel started to move. After a few revolutions, I heard a loud hiss of air. Popping open, it revealed a stretch of hallway, steel rivets encircling the narrow tunnel. Small circles of illumination dotted the ceiling. A tract of soiled grating weaved a path towards some far off destination hid by the curvature of the tunnel. Pipes ran along the walls, but these were different than what I'd seen before. There were thick ones and thin ones, some more brass colored, while others were coal gray. I stumbled forward, my legs so tired by this point that I could feel a constant twinge of pain in my thighs. The tunnel twisted and turned and seemed to go on forever. At a few points I debated going back.

But what if that nullified whatever the girl had done for me? Was this where she meant for me to go? Had I made a mistake by veering off the first path? Was she going to meet me here? Were there more of those things like the one she had killed?

The tunnel rounded a turn and ended at what looked like an ancient elevator. There was a single brass button, but no markings. I pressed the button and the doors opened. A metal safety gate, like the old elevators I had seen in history books, blocked my entry. Reaching out, I pulled it up. With a metallic screech it rolled into the ceiling.

Inside the elevator looked antique and classy. I glanced back down the hall. Silent as a grave.

Holy shit! The floors went up to 200! The building I entered didn't look nearly that tall!

The doors closed, and the elevator started ascending without me touching anything. Leaning against the far wall, I drew in a deep breath.

A WHOLE WORLD

Ten minutes passed, maybe more, and finally the elevator ground to a shaky halt. I backed into the corner, wishing I had a knife or something. I might have made a big mistake by getting in this thing. The doors opened with a hiss, revealing, to my surprise, the last thing in the world I expected to see.

It looked like the sitting room in an old house. Dark paneled oak walls, Victorian wooden chairs, and a marble-topped coffee table centered on a crimson rug. Brass candelabra garnished the walls, the tips alive in flickering flames. Before me was an ornate desk topped by a strange, boxy looking thing embossed by brass groves that resembled rib bones.

What was this place?

"You probably have a lot of questions, Aaron."

My heart jumped into my throat. Casually emerging from the corner, sharply dressed as ever, was that man from DC.

"Have a seat."

He pulled out a chair.

"You've been doing quite a bit of jumping about, haven't you?"

I looked at him quizzically, and he smirked.

"You don't even know that you're doing it, do you?

"We've had to directly intervene twice now, just to save your life."

I kept staring at him, not sure what to say.

"And you're not making it any easier."

His pauses were drawn out. Like an accusation. Or maybe he expected me to say something.

"There's more than one party that thinks they would be better off just getting rid of you."

He paused again, still staring calmly.

"Personally, we have a little more of a delicate, wait and see approach."

"We? Who is this we?"

"The million-dollar question. Isn't that how you say it?"

I shrugged my shoulders.

"Maybe you are a bit too young for that."

He leaned forward.

"It doesn't matter. What is important is that you realize what you are doing, and who is coming after you. Like I told you back in Washington, D.C., you have a special gift. You can't control it right now, and your erratic actions are throwing up warning signals. Some are... less patient that we are."

Again, he paused. The intensity of his gaze was unsettling.

"Your own people are probably the biggest threat. They are a bit crude in their understanding and are leaning towards just getting rid of the problem. There are dissenting voices, but they are losing. It's only because of those elements that they let you go in the first place. I doubt they'll do that again."

Before I could catch myself, I leaned forward and blurted out...

"But why me?"

I felt stupid. My face flushed, and I remained frozen, too embarrassed to even sit back. The man showed no reaction, still looking at me with that same cool intensity.

"You walk between worlds, Aaron. At first, you only communicated with them. Now, you travel to them as well."

He paused for a moment, as if to let that sink in.

The threats on my life were new. Or were they? Maybe they had been there all along? His friendliness before— friendliness wasn't quite the right word. Civility? Politeness?

Did he drug me back in DC? He gave me his card. Was that a trick? A ruse to gain my confidence? Maybe he had helped me out. Maybe not."

"It doesn't matter if you believe me. If you want to live, you'll pay attention. Your government is afraid you will bring something back. Something from another world. A virus. Unfriendly forces. They aren't sure, but the current debate centers around whether they should try to use or kill you."

Was he reading my thoughts?

"Yes"

Fuck!

"If I wanted to kill you, I could have done it at any time. Your people are trying to keep tabs on you, but you've made that such a risky proposition that if they get a hold of you again, I'm not sure what they will do."

"You said my people are the biggest threat? Who are my people? And what else is a threat?"

I meant that to sound more normal, but my voice betrayed me. It sounded tinny, like a child's voice.

"Your race, Aaron. You are from one small planet in a giant cosmos. A backwards planet that is still riddled with internal strife. Some species are even more backwards than yours. The ones capable of interstellar flight often compete with other species they encounter. There are many different lines of thought. You are an abnormality in a very complex game. Your gift is dangerous, but intriguing. Many would like to control it, but plenty would rather eliminate it rather than let you fall into another's hands."

Was he telling me the truth? If he was, why did he look so... human? And what about the antique clothing, colloquialisms, and all that?

"We have been studying your species since you were crawling out of caves and wearing animal skins. I look like this because we assumed it would be more acceptable to you. It appeared that your people, as a species, invest more trust in this era of human society than in any other in the last century."

Fuck, he's reading my mind again!

"You can learn how to guard your thoughts. That might be for the best."

"So, what are you? Why should I trust you when you've been lying to me since day one?"

That was a bold move, but his face didn't change. I could swear he was amused by me.

"Compared to you, we are a very old race. Your people are curious by nature, but they think, and not without reason, that you could be a great risk."

He paused, picked up a thin, metal cylinder, and turned it over in his fingers.

"By agreement, your planet is off limits. But only in this dimension. It has been invaded and ravaged in others. You just came from one. The girl, who you impregnated incidentally, killed several M'ddi. Things have become... complicated."

Pregnant? How does he even know that?

He rose from the desk and pushed in the chair.

"Let me show you something."

He rose and walked to the curtains. Parting them, a bright light swept in. I climbed out of the chair and stumbled forward.

Spreading out before me was an endless cityscape, the buildings so tall their upper echelons disappeared into the clouds. The sun was setting, breaking across the horizon in brilliant streams of orange and yellow. The edifices were strangely angled, their windows framed portals of rounded glass. Tubes flowed in and out of the buildings in a mesh of latticed metal structures. Soot-stained exhaust ports swarmed the rooftops. A flurry of strange oval craft floated darted about.

"Is... is this earth?"

"Oh, no. It is similar, in a lot of ways. The inhabitant's breath air, and communicate in a verbal language, but this planet is smaller, revolves around distant twin stars, and the physiology of its inhabitants is quite different."

"What... why am I here?"

"Because you have no control over what you are doing, and this is where you ended up. So far, you have somehow managed to travel to destinations that can support your life form. The reasons behind that aren't quite clear, but there is danger here, and you need guidance. This planet is probably going to be destroyed. They pollute heavily, have taxed their natural resources beyond recovery, and have covered the surface of this planet with an endless megalopolis. They've now ventured out into space to sustain themselves, strip mining everything their nascent technology can reach. They are seen as a parasite, one that will soon be intruding into territories claimed by others."

This more and more resembled a dream. Like most dreams, it seemed incredibly real, at least up until the end, when reason and proximity to wakefulness would seep in.

"This is very real. Your life is in your hands, and you need to make up your mind on what you are going to do. You have wandered into a viral outbreak, impregnated a girl, and stumbled into a polluted backwater that is likely to be destroyed at any moment. Too long here, and you will perish with this world. If you return to the wrong place on your home planet, you'll be imprisoned and subjected to experiments. If someone like the M'ddi come across you, they will most likely kill you. They already tried."

He reached over and pulled the curtains closed. As the drapes folded in, shutting out the glare, I got my first clear look at the patterns. They weren't the floral designs I presumed at all, but more closely resembled fossilized sea creatures. Pointing at the elevator, the man broke my train of thought.

"Take the elevator down to the first floor. When you get off, you will be back on earth. Come to my office. We'll talk."

I stared at him.

"We have little time left. Go. Now."

Taking a deep breath, I headed toward the elevator. As I passed, I absently glanced over at the wall. Elegant frames bracketed portraits of strange, heavily wrinkled humanoid.

"Quickly."

Stepping into the elevator, the doors closed, and without touching anything, it started to descend.

THE COLLAPSE OF SOCIETY

The doors opened to reveal a sight I had seen in the wealthier parts of DC. Highly polished marble floors. Whitewashed pillars. Giant silver-framed windows. An empty reception desk sat in front of me. All the interior lights were off.

Was it the weekend?

An immense crack shook the floor. It sounded again, farther away this time, and I ran to the glass front doors and pulled on the handle.

Locked!

I looked back in a panic. Dark halls receded to the left and right, the metal box of an EXIT sign mounted in between. It wasn't lit, which I thought was mandatory, but I turned and ran for it regardless. Below the exit sign were the dim features of a metal door. Glancing down the darkened hallways I turned back to the door. The boom sounded again. My footing was less solid this time, and the resounding vibration pitched me into the door. Scampering back up I smashed my palms into the lever. The door flew open, and I tumbled out.

I could make out the silhouette of a guard rail and some stairs. Grasping the metal rail, I slowly made it down several steps. The guardrail ended, and the floor leveled out. I let go and blundered forward, the darkness now absolute. My hand brushed against something, and I pulled back instinctively, then extended it again. Deciding it must be the lever of a fire door, I gave it a push. Blinding sunlight poured in, and I let go of the door to cover my eyes.

A wide sidewalk spread before me. Blinking, I could make out the blur of a two-lane street. Strangely, there were no cars. Maybe this was a weekend, and the business district was vacant? Another thunderclap sounded, louder than before, and the ground beneath me shook. I steadied myself and wandered out into the middle of the street. The staccato noise of gunfire brought me to full attention, and I sprinted for the opposite building. I made it over the curb, up onto the sidewalk, and almost into the shadow of an overhanging balustrade when the car engine resonated, immediately followed by another burst of gunfire. I dove the last few steps into the shade, trying to roll as my forearms slammed down against the concrete, the sleeves of my jacket grounding across the pavement.

Fuck! I saved up for three months to buy that jacket!

More gunfire erupted, closer this time. As I glanced around, I saw that large buildings sidled the road, their lower reaches obscured by a thin morning fog. Popping around a bend, the front of a blue pickup emerged, the silhouette of a man, rifle aloft in hand, clearly visible in the back. His back turned to me, he let off another burst, a cascade of shells erupting. There was another loud crack, and the rear end of the pickup raised in a ball of fire. The man in the truck bed dove out and hurtled straight at me.

I scurried to the side, slamming into the glass of a large door just as the man plowed into the pavement. Forehead skidding into the concrete, his cranium exploded in a burst of blood and gore. I fought back the urge to vomit as I backed along the glass but couldn't pull my eyes away. A huge wallop erupted behind me, and I whirled around to see that the pickup truck had smashed into the building across the street, its overturned carcass now engulfed in flames. The ground under my boots started vibrating, and a hulking silhouette emerged.

A fucking tank!

I pushed off the wall and started running, darting across the street and into the overhanging shade. There was an explosion behind, and shards of rock pelted my body, throwing me into a tumble across the pavement. Scraping my palms on the asphalt as I rolled over, I scrambled back up, my hands now raw and on fire. I glanced over my shoulder and could see that the building was missing a huge chunk from its wall, the lower window now a fire-belching black hole. I poured on as much of my fading energy as I could muster. Crossing the last blocks of concrete, I burst out into the brilliance of a wide cross-street. A streetlamp's top erupted in a ball of fire and my arms flew up in an attempt to shield me from the debris. Chunks pelted my legs and coat. Gasping for air, my hands still shielding my face, I pounded the pavement, trying to keep my head down as I ran. The wall behind the lamp broke out in a queue of splintered bursts, the staccato boom of a fifty-caliber thumping through the air.

My lungs were on fire. The nearby fence door was slightly ajar, and I scrambled for it. Hurdling a concrete beam I climbed over a cloth barrier, lost my footing, and tumbled into an earthen pit. Crawling to my feet, streaked by dirt, I looked up to see the overhanging arms of a construction crane. A thunderclap pushed me back again, the overhanging arm bursting into a fireball. A deafening roar rumbled close behind, the shockwaves of it slamming me backwards. I struggled to my feet, the shifting sand and gravel underfoot fighting me every step of the way. As I looked up, I saw that the charred arm of the crane was breaking loose.

Fuck! Fuck! Fuck!

My overwrought scrambling worked against me, tearing loose rock and soil as it conspired to keep me from moving. I shifted course, turned around, and tried to run down the hill. I tripped and rolled, my jacket whipping about me as a trail of dust kicked up in my wake. The ground shook, a roiling boom following it as the arm of the crane smashed into the earth. I sprung sideways just moments before the mass of metal smashed into the ground. Looking around wildly, I saw a rising slope and headed for it.

I had almost made it when the barrier at the top erupted in splintered bursts. I was sure I was going to die. I kept scrambling, but I was losing ground, the rocks and sand fighting me every step of the way. Gunfire erupted again, and I huddled down, covering my head with my hands. Only this time, there was no burst of wood. In fact, despite the ringing in my ears, the bursts sounded slightly different. Less powerful.

Maybe it was more of those people in that truck!

I gathered my bearings and as I crested the top, a chain-link fence greeted me. There was probably a better exit somewhere, but I had my break, and I wasn't going to waste it searching for an exit. Scaling the fence, I dropped over the supporting barriers and into the middle of a street. I peered left and right and could see that I was now in the middle of an empty four-lane highway. Jogging across, I bounded onto the sidewalk. A giant glass building was not far away. That would be the Watergate Hotel. I knew where I was.

I suddenly thought to look back for the tank. I could see the lot, the bright blue billboards advertising the construction firms. But no movement.

Then there was another burst of gunfire and I sidled up to the nearby building as I headed toward the nearest cross-street. A traffic lamppost was just ahead, its beacons unlit. Beyond was a street sign and I headed for it, instinctively watching for traffic that wasn't there.

10th Street Northwest! And the cross-street was New York Avenue!

That put me close to K Street. DC always struck me as nauseatingly bland. Even the trees decorating the sidewalks were fenced in and micromanaged. Only the absolute desolation tainted the wholesome ambiance.

What was going on?

I reached the opposite corner, and sure enough, the sign read "9th Street." Turning in, the left blossomed out into a large, grassy lawn.

This didn't look like the downtown DC I remembered. Then again, I never came to this area. The rich people here would call the police on me before I made it two feet.

I ran through a maze of giant urns overflowing with greenery and wove in and out of tables sprouting blue umbrellas. All in an attempt to stay close to the buildings.

Where was I? I had just left Ninth so I should be headed toward Tenth.

I was on the correct side of the street for odd letters, but this all looked glossy and commercial. I distinctly remembered an old, wooden door.

There were shiny storefront windows, the awnings marking them as Metropolitan News and the like, and all were part of a giant building labeled 901 New York. Right beside the main door was an entrance for an underground parking lot, but there was no sign of the door I was looking for.

What the fuck?

Giving the parking garage a wide berth, I sidled up next to what I thought was a Starbucks, only the green awning turned out to be a deception. It was a childcare facility. I ran my fingers along the wall in disbelief. My head was turned, and I was viewing the opposite side of the street when my probing hand lost its grip, and I toppled into the stone wall. Only it wasn't a wall.

A SHIFT IN PRIORITIES

As I righted myself, I looked around in wonder. Light was filtering in from on high, the air a dusty soup of floating particles. It all smelled like an old basement. A soiled concrete floor led to a much-abused staircase. I started toward the stairs, and my vision wavered. The hallway transformed into the space I remembered, but only momentarily. So brief in fact, that I wondered if I had really seen it. The stairs creaked under foot, one so cracked and chipped it flexed precariously.

At the top was another door, and this looked like it belonged in a barn. There was no visible handle, so I leaned into the door. It didn't budge. I rammed my shoulder into it. With a creak, it broke open and I fell forward. Regaining my balance with the help of a desktop, I looked about at what was now a slightly better lit office. My palm started sliding. I yanked it back and noticed that everything was covered in a layer of silt. Pale light poured through slat blinds. I could make out the remnants of what looked more or less like that office I had been in, only now aged and untouched for decades. The same wooden furniture, candlestick phone, and typewriter, but now buried under a coat of dust, and entangled in tattered clusters of spider webs. A coat rack in the corner held a charcoal fedora and trench coat, partially obscuring a cracked plaster wall. Then everything around me seemed to ripple. It all warmed in tone, the dull gray shifting into warmer hues.

"So Aaron…"

I spun around.

It was that same man. He was seated, legs were crossed, his fedora tilted so it hid most of the face. One of his fingers was curled over his lip, as though he was buried in thought. I took the seat opposite him.

"Things have changed. Quite a bit actually. Your world is in turmoil, and we're debating what to do with you."

"What do you mean… debating…"

"Oh, we aren't going to get rid of you. But like I said, you're a loose cannon. At first, the traits you exhibited were interesting, if not remarkable. That has changed."

"I… what?"

"You have moved forward more than a year from when I saw you last."

"What, a few minutes ago?"

"Two years have passed since you left your world. It was a jump of a month or two at first, but that pace has quickened. You know nothing of this?"

Everything was getting weirder by the minute. The old-school vibe. The appearing at all the right times.

"Like I told you, we thought this approach would comfort you."

Goddammit! He's reading my mind again! I need to... I don't know—

"You need to screen your thoughts. I told you that already. Yes, you are seeing what we thought would be the best. To gain your confidence. You should realize that we do not want you to come to any harm."

"What now?"

He stared at me, suddenly raising his hand and pointing up. Signaling, I think, that he heard something.

"Someone has the...suit...now. Your case has become... less important."

"The suit?"

"One of your own, apparently."

"What suit?"

His expression didn't change, but I could swear he was chuckling.

"You wouldn't understand, but this has become a major incident. It would be unfair to completely abandon you. We'll... we'll see."

And just like that he disappeared, the color leaching out of the room with him. Cold, damp air seeped in, and the temperature started to drop. I rose, glancing at the desk as I did so, and recoiled. Seated in the chair was the skeleton of a man. Folds of a dress shirt flowed over rib bones; a skull half buried under a fedora. I looked around. The room seemed to have grown into a disheveled storeroom that extended out through a mass of worktables. All the tables were roughly the same size, their surfaces mired with a throng of cardboard boxes. Beyond them I could see what looked like a door.

Navigating between the tables, some so close together I had to duck under and squeeze between shadowy legs, I made it to the door.

The handle was hidden behind a mountain of boxes. I craned up to reach the top one and slapped at the sides. After a few tries it toppled. As I lowered a second box and was lifting a third the tape on the bottom gave way, dumping a swarm of papers on me. I squatted and picked up the first sheet. A little heavier than notebook paper, it had a thin, plastic feel. The light was dim, but the writing on it looked like the Sumerian runes I had seen in history books. I set it aside and picked up another sheet. More of the same. I shuffled through the pile and a page with illustrations grabbed my eye. Pulling it out, I could see that it was a map of sorts. It showed what appeared to be the earth at various evolutionary stages. The first images a single land mass that slowly morphed with each following drawing into a series of more modern disbursements. A low moan sounded, and I froze.

THE DANGERS ALL AROUND US

The moan sounded again, the hairs on the back of my neck prickling. Something, a primal instinct, warned me to run. I scrambled to my feet, pawing at the boxes and sending them flying as I tried to dig out the door handle. Dust clogged the air, ushering in a fit of coughing, but I didn't dare slow down. Sweat rolled into my eye, blurring my vision. The shadowy form of a doorknob materialized, and my desperation increased. The moan, louder this time, sounded again, and I tore at the remaining boxes, leaning against them with all my might.

The handle was now mostly free, and I grabbed at it, turning and pushing.

The door didn't budge!

I gave the handle a hard pull and it cracked open slightly, a stream of blueish light streaking in.

Fuck!

I yanked on the door, twisting my torso and kicking at boxes. It opened a little more, and I tried to squeeze through.

Not wide enough!

I slammed the heel of my boot into the boxes and pulled with all my might on the lip of the door. It edged a little wider, and as I squeezed through my jacket caught. I frantically pawed at the edges, then let it go as I wriggled into the hallway beyond.

All polished and glossy, the marble floors fought against my stability as I tried to steady myself. I managed to stop sliding and whirled around to see that the door was gone.

This place appeared to be a downtown office building, and it looked like I was in the reception area. The ground shook, followed by a thunderclap and the crackling of glass. A shockwave resounded, a torrent of glass shards pelting the wall. The thump of automatic fire followed. I started running into the recesses of the hall. Darkness closed in and I slowed, my outstretched arm feeling for any invisible barricade. The ground under my feet mutated into something lumpy and textured. I hit an outcropping and almost fell, breaking my fall with an awkward stumble. Grit assailed my eyes, and as I paused to wipe my face I noticed a damp, earthen smell.

How could that possibly be... unless I had wandered into a basement. But the hall had been straight, and I hadn't detected any decline.

I kicked at the floor and my toecap sunk in. Squatting, I ran my palms over the surface. Cool, damp earth.

What the fuck? Had I traveled again?

I rose and stumbled forward blindly. Time grew vague, and the next thing I registered was when my fingertips bumped into something. Instinctively jerking back, I slowly reached out toward whatever was in front of me.

It seemed to be a wall of stone, the rough surface sinking into groves that must be the division between blocks. There were openings on the right and left, but movement forward was blocked. I turned left at random, running my hand along the wall as I proceeded.

With slow, deliberate steps, the ground beneath me eventually leveled out. After a few minutes, the ambient light increased, the walls now visibly marked with strangely painted designs. The pathway curved and opened into a small cavern. A massive sinkhole occupied most of the floor. Six small globes encircled it, crackles of light snapping out of the black maw.

What the fuck was this?

I approached the rim and looked around for something to prod with.

Nothing.

Kneeling, I ran my palm across the ground. Dust rose in small flurries but that was it. I dug a little harder, my fingertips scratching into the loosely packed soil, and alighted on something. Scooting a little closer, I brushed away the dirt and grooved patterns emerged. I cleared a little more and unearthed a swath of what looked like a buried stone floor. A few pebbles littered the dirt and I scooped up a couple. Tossing one into the swirling abyss, a crack of light leaped out, followed by a ripple on the surface.

I tossed another. Then another. Same thing. I tossed the remaining few at once. Little bursts of light were accompanied by a network of ripples. I debated delving my hand in. I extended my index finger but stopped just shy of the surface.

What if I lost my finger?

I stood there trying to decide what to do for what must have been a half-hour. I stepped a little closer to the rift and then stepped back

Fuck! Fuck! Fuck!

Raising my arm I edged forward, squinting my eyes as if I could pretend I wasn't really doing this.

It didn't feel like liquid, but it was thicker than air. My fingertip sank in slightly, and there was an electric tingle. I leaned forward, my finger delving in as the miasma around it rippled in small eddies. Then something grabbed my hand and wrenched me forward.

IT ALL GOES TO HELL

Acrackling swirl of murkiness washed over me. The air grew thin, and my arm felt like it was being wrenched out of its socket.

I landed with a heavy thump. A smog of grit churned about me, the chalkiness of it working into my mouth and eyes. I tried to gulp air, but it felt thin. My lips scraped over the sheen of dust coating my teeth as I gasped. Pain seared through my shoulder as something tugged ferociously at my arm.

I was being dragged forward.

I blinked, the shadow enough now that I could make out a starry sky. Dunes of sand and rose on all sides, the bulk of looming cliffs visible across an ocean of white. I tried to twist around and see what had ahold of me, and caught a glimpse of something slimy and green, its cord-like tentacles wrapped around my forearm. I started twisting, trying to break loose, but the tendrils enveloping my arm tightened. My squirming erupted into a feverish thrashing, my heart jumping into my chest as I started to cough and choke. I felt lightheaded and opened my mouth to scream, but nothing came out. Then, with an incredible flash, I heard a horrible shriek.

Everything went black.

I woke up with a start, lunging forward into a crouch. The edges of my vision were still blurry, and I gasped. My ribs felt tight and bruised, my back knotted up, and my head ached. I bent over and hurled. As I cradled my head, I shook it gently and slowly opened my eyes.

I was in that graveyard in Virginia!

It looked just like I remembered. Neutered trees, their lower limbs carefully pruned to give them an air of servility. Conservatively groomed bushes. Bundles of cut flowers holstered symmetrically on paths of asphalt. A hot midday sun beat down relentlessly, augmenting my aches and pains. Then out of the corner of my eye I saw something that made my blood run cold. It was small and child-like, with oversized black orbs for eyes. Then, in a quick blur, it was gone.

Was it a hallucination?

I struggled to my feet and shook my head. As I grunted with the pain of standing upright, I trudged forward.

Should I go back home? Head to my friend's house? Everything looked so... normal again. Then I realized I no longer had my skateboard. At the very least I should head home and get some sort of ride. Another board, or a bike.

I heard a thunderclap and fell to my knees. Something roared above, and I looked up to see the contrails of a squadron of aircraft. I debated what to do. My friend at least had a car. And a gun. My shoulders sagged as I stared at the ground in resignation. Well, he was my best bet. I headed for the road, knowing it would take almost an hour on foot.

Every minute seemed like an eternity, but I felt too wiped out to go any faster. Placid suburbia flowed by. It all looked so affectless. So... middle American. The lawns were carefully culled to make the trees, bushes, and all-important grass landscape look as neutered and subdued as possible.

God, I hated Fairfax!

The houses looked abandoned and shuttered, but they always did at midday. Like no one really lived here, they just returned to their pet dog park to sleep.

A good twenty minutes passed, and I noticed there were no cars on the road. Actually, there were no cars in most of the driveways. That was odd. The sidewalk ended and I skipped across the street, scanning instinctively for traffic, but the highway remained empty. My friend's road, Stroughton, as demarcated by a green sign, popped up on the left. I followed, the sidewalk disintegrating into a strip of trampled grass. A few steps led up to his driveway. I stopped and looked at the lowly brick building. There was a crimson minivan perched in the driveway. Someone was home.

No sign of movement in the house, but then again, there never was. He lived with his grandparents. Grumpy old folks who had long since retired. While it was still light outside, he was usually asleep, or melded to his computer. He rarely had a job during the summer. His blue Monte Carlo was still perched in the bend of the driveway. Everything seemed calm now. Normal. Like this had all been a figment of my imagination.

He'd laugh. Ask me what I was on.

A shadowy wave rolled across the front lawn, throwing a stretch of shadows over the stone water fountain. The sky was darkening, thunderclouds roiling and twisting into aggregates of deep purple. Spurts of intense light crackled through.

Was it going to rain?

That spurred me on, and I headed for the front door. I tapped on the glass, but no one responded. I banged again, harder this time. Still nothing. A chill overcame me, and I glanced behind. The ground was almost invisible now, a pale mist having swooped in. The sky continued its crackling, writhing into an ever more threatening morass. Then the noises started.

They were faint at first, and I strained my hearing to make sure they were real. The fog was really pouring in now and I could see a thicker mass of it drifting toward me. A noise sounded again, deep and rolling, like the bellowing of some animal. The hairs on the back of my neck stood up and I frantically grabbed the knob.

It was open!

Twisting the handle, I slipped in.

His house always smelled like old people. K-Mart cheapo air freshener mingled with a subtle scent of decay. The interior was dark and musty. The living room on my right brandished a brown couch that fronted the kitchen counter. Everything was dark, the sunlight shut out by thick curtains. It looked like it always did, although the grandparents were usually milling about. Everything was quiet. Too quiet. I glanced down Tommy's hallway. Grandma might be in her room, but granddad was usually out here. He slept on a cot in the garage. Tommy said his grandma complained that he farted too much. I was drifting into a reverie when I heard a slight groan and froze. I started backing toward the front door, and then remembered what had driven me inside. I chewed on my lip and looked about anxiously. A scuffling followed, and I sidled up closer to the front door.

This had been a mistake.

A throaty hacking was accompanied by a thump and sharp cry of pain.

That sounded like Tommy's grandmother!

I was torn between an urge to help her and an impulse to run.

I didn't even like her! She gave me dirty looks and barely talked to me!

"Now, now, Aaron... let's not do anything hasty."

I snapped my head around. Standing between the kitchen counter and front wall was one of the agents from the police station. The smaller, sleazier looking one. He was wearing the same black suit, slightly more disheveled, and holding aloft a pistol.

"What... I don't..."

"I get the sneaking suspicion that you are somehow involved in all of this. And the best part? I don't even think

you're aware of it. But you know what else? I don't give a fuck."

"I... I don't... Look, I just stumbled into this... whatever this is. I didn't do anything."

He slowly approached; gun still held aloft.

"It doesn't really matter what you say, kid. No more running. No more hiding. "

He grinned, his thin lips peeling back to reveal teeth that looked too numerous to fit in such a small mouth.

"It's checkmate, kid. You're coming with me. What you have, it's real special. You probably don't even know how special it is. We're dealing with big issues. Craziness. And I think you'll play a real important part of who comes out on top."

He smiled again. With that slimy, creepy sneer.

"It's for the best. You'll probably be safer."

There was a scraping noise behind him, and I glanced down to see Tommy's grandpa. His arms and legs were tied behind his back, a red cloth stuffed in his mouth. He was scuttling across the tile floor, clearly headed for the garage. The man turned, gun arm swinging toward the huddled form, and an explosion rang out. I covered my head and cowed, the burst pounding into my skull and starting a ringing in my ears. As I was dropping, the agent's head exploded.

Strings of blood and bits of brain splattered across the wall, a mist of gore descending. A revolting, warm animal smell filled the air, making me instantly nauseous. His headless body remained standing for a moment, then crumpled, the stumpy remains of the neck colliding with the wall and leaving a grisly streak as it slid down.

"Fuck..."

I spun to my left.

"Tommy!"

He looked half-asleep. Slightly shocked, slightly indifferent, a smoking revolver still in his hand.

"You killed him!"

"No shit."

"But... what are we going to do..."

"I dunno. I just woke up."

With that he let his gun arm fall limply to his side, turned around, and headed back to his room. As he turned the corner, I heard a muffled yelp and turned back to see grandpa, still huddled on the ground, arms thrashing and twitching about. I darted over and undid his ropes. As he pulled the gag from his mouth, he shot me a dirty look. I turned in disgust and headed toward Tommy's room.

IT'S ALL SHIT ANYWAYS

Sitting in his leather office chair, Tommy stared vacantly at the computer monitor. Only his pale face was visible, but it looked like he had been crying.

"Tommy."

He wouldn't look at me.

"Tommy!"

Nothing.

"*Tommy!*"

Without turning, he snapped-

"What?"

"Tommy. What do you want to do?"

His tone was almost a deadpan mumble.

"About what?"

"About all this! Have you been outside? Have you seen the news? The world is falling apart!"

Nothing.

"Tommy?"

Without even turning, he muttered-

"All right. All right. Grab my knife. It's in the bottom drawer. We'll take the Monte Carlo."

"Where to?"

"I don't know. Blacksburg. There's a group house down there."

I headed over to the small chest-of-drawers.

"Bottom drawer."

Pulling it open, I rummaged among some T-shirts and pulled out a Kabar. Undoing my belt, I attached the sheath.

"You have a sweatshirt I can use?"

"What happened to your leather jacket? You always have that thing."

"It's a long story."

"Yeah, middle drawer. Don't take my Slayer one."

I pulled out an Agnostic Front "boots and braces" hoodie.

"All right, c'mon."

Tommy had risen to his feet and was zipping up the thin, old-man-style leather jacket he always wore. His gaunt face stared at me indifferently for a moment. Then he swiveled around, raising the handgun in front like he was cop on TV, and edged around the corner. I pulled the knife from its sheath and followed.

His grandparents were not in the living room. Tommy crept over to the front door and cracked it open. A sliver of white shot in. Tommy blinked, and with the gun still held aloft, he pulled open the door. The fog was gone and now it was bright and clear outside. I stood stupefied for a moment, then realized Tommy was already in the car. I scurried over and dove in as Tommy peeled out. I didn't really know these people in Blacksburg. I had been there once, briefly, crashing on their floor with my friends at a party. Still, rural Virginia had to be safer than a metropolitan hub like DC.

We skidded left onto Burke Station Road, took a right onto Main Street, and headed toward 66. Walls of trees flew by, a few houses nestled among them, but not a single car was on the road. Apocalypse, here we come. I slunk down in my seat and wondered if this was really worse. 9 to 5, you're not alive. And at least I was still alive. Or I thought I was.

EYE DEEP IN HELL

PROLOGUE

A war hospital, Flanders, France. March 1919.

"Any ID on the poor man yet?"

"I think he's from one of the London Territorial Battalions. Bit hard to tell in his present condition."

"He still hasn't uttered a word?"

"No. There are plenty of these boys, unfortunately. The shell shock seems to render them mute. "Poor wretched things just drool and stare at the wall."

"The pity is that the war was almost over when it happened. Where was he found again?"

"In what they call "no man's land". The villagers noticed him stumbling aimlessly between the trenches."

"Where was he all that time? The war ended months ago."

"I don't have a clue. They said he mumbled something unintelligible and hasn't said a word since."

"What was it?"

"It was, oh dear, I'm trying to remember... I think they said he was wild eyed, trying to warn them about something, but unfortunately his mind was too far gone. *'Beware the Germans...?* No, that wasn't quite it..."

"That's not a surprise, although it's pretty unlikely that the Germans will ever pose a threat again."

"Yeah, it's too bad he's not around to see it. I don't think anyone back home knows what they went through."

EYE DEEP IN HELL

The grime was like a living thing. Cold and filthy as it coated my skin. I hadn't bathed in over a month, and the trench was nothing but mud. It worked its way into everything. Between the scratchy, dirt-encrusted layers of canvas swaddled around my legs and pooling up between my toes. I could barely feel them anymore, cold numbness bypassing the initial burning sting. I pictured them in my mind, the blackness of frostbite creeping in. As I slogged through knee-deep muck, the rising stink intermingled with the decay of humanity.

I didn't know what it was like to be fully alive anymore. I spent every day in a sleep-deprived daze. Slouching up against a wall of dirt, I often tried to catch a wink or two. The moist cold creeped in at every point my clothing thinned, and that seemed to be almost everywhere. Even my sweat had saturated the cloth to the point where it felt stiff and caustic, entangling my body in filthy strips of sandpaper marauding as cotton.

The fear was constant, a condition that over time settled into an ongoing state of tension and misery. And apathy. Sometimes you could hear the death groans of those stranded amidst the barbed wire in no man's land. It used to make me sad, but I'd grown to despise it. To wish them all a quicker death. The stench of their blood filled the air, making it even more vile, the sounds like nails on a chalkboard. It had been raining for days, the storm abating only hours ago, and the sky was still dark with roiling clouds. I couldn't find my regiment. They were here a minute ago. At least I thought it was a minute. It'd been so long since I'd had more than a couple hours of sleep, I was starting to doubt my capacity to reason.

Shadows emerged at the corners of my vision, dark shapes that flitted across the decaying walls, only to disappear as I swiveled toward them. Overhead gusts of haze rolled by, the smells of gunpowder and decaying flesh drifting down. I couldn't tell you who was left, maybe less than a half-dozen of us. We went over the top days ago. Bullets were flying in a rain of metal from the machine guns of the Huns. We were dropping like flies. The man in front head exploded, a cascade of blood and gore pelting me in clumps of brain matter. I started retching, curling downwards in an attempt to keep the vomit off my clothes. Maybe that saved me. I don't know. I made it to the next trench, my feet buckling as I fell in. I could swear I saw others join me. Men falling in tangled hordes as smoke and airborne clumps of mud obscured everything. I think shrapnel hit my backpack, as now it's sporting a jagged hole. It didn't lighten the load, but I'm sure it tore into something that will make my life even worse down the road. I staggered just a few feet through the trench when the sky darkened more, and the rain started up again. The soil beneath my feet deteriorated into a watery slime that pulled at my boots. My right foot slid, and I threw out my hand in an attempt to break the fall. My open palm slammed into a muddy wall and sank in. My fingers clutched something, and I tried to tighten my grip around it. But it was to no avail, as whatever I grabbed onto pulled out of the muck, and I stumbled backwards. The damp ground did little to break my fall, and I landed hard on my left hip. My rifle thumped heavily as the butt hit the ground, jerking the strap around my neck into a tourniquet. My fingers were still caught in something, and as I pulled them into view, I let out a string of curses. A partially decayed head, its stringy wisps of beard still adorning the jawline, broke free and spun down on me in a blurry mess of peeling flesh and eyeless sockets.

Fuck!

I spent a few moments trying to scramble to my feet, rubbing my hand fiercely against my wool overcoat as the soles of my boots slipped in the mud. I managed to scramble up against the far wall as I glanced around for my helmet. But it was to no avail.

Was that a German or one of ours?

It was too decayed to tell, and now it was too dark to see anything. I kept moving.

I didn't know where I was, where my company was, or what was left of them, but staying still was death. I shuddered, hunched my shoulders together in an effort to gain a little warmth, and trundled forward.

ANOTHER DAY, WORSE THAN THE ONE BEFORE

The cool vapor of moist earth awoke me. It looked like the middle of the night, but I couldn't be sure of the time. I must have passed out. Last I remembered, my fingers had come across a wooden outcropping jutting from the wall, and I followed it until I stumbled on a subterranean chamber. It was completely dark, which probably meant it was empty, but I was so close to passing out, I didn't care. I don't remember curling up in the corner, but I must have because I was uncurling now.

With my short sleep, I was colder than ever, and had to shake the feeling back into my fingers. I felt around for my rifle, and my fingers brushed over the cold metal barrel.

I didn't hear the patter of rain outside anymore, only a shrill whistling. Probably from the wind whipping over the trench.

With a loud crack, I was bathed in brilliance. The noise picked up and started pelting me in waves. I stumbled backwards, my stomach churning as blood trickled from my ears.

There must be an artillery bombardment.

A shock wave hit me, and I lost my footing, falling backwards on my already sore hip. Something hard under the mud slammed into my leg, and I howled in pain. Tears welled up in my eyes and I folded over, rocking to and fro in misery. The bright flashes eventually faded, leaving a lingering glow on my retina. I struggled to my feet, grabbed my rifle, and hobbled over to the doorway. Only a frame of roughly cut wood, I placed a hand on one edge and peered out.

The trench flowed by in a long, muddy corridor. If they were shelling the area, an attack was probably eminent. Stumbling out, I shuffled down the trench.

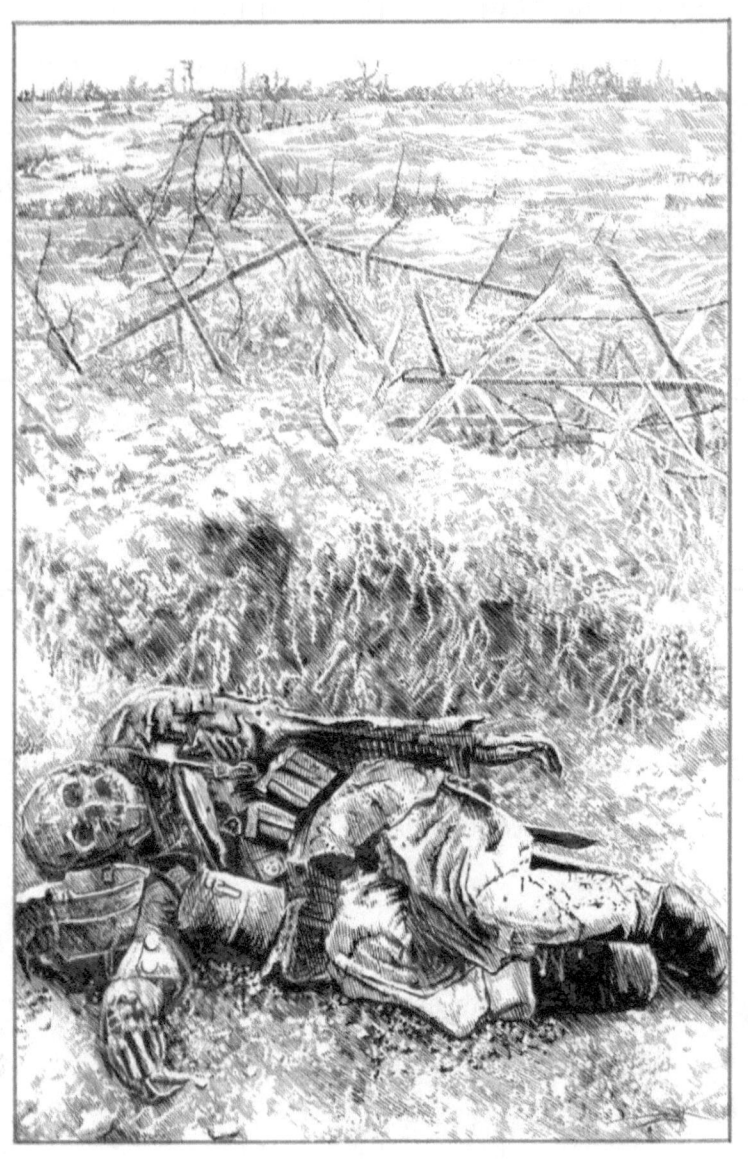

A MAZE OF HORRORS

None of the trenches were straight lines, lest a machine gunner drop down and mow through a battalion of sitting ducks. Necessary, but that made them a rat's maze. I ducked under arches of timber, rounded corners of protruding rock, and stumbled across my first corpses.

Within a few feet the corridor widened into a long path that twisted downward. The morning light was approaching, transforming the sky into a pale gray. I could see the shadowy forms of dead men ahead, their prone bodies half buried in the mud. As I drew up on the men, I noticed that the walkway beneath my feet was growing firmer, almost like a loose layer of dirt blanked a cobblestone trail. Hard to see much in the hazy light, but I thought I could make out the glimmer of a worn stone or two beneath the mud.

That was strange. Who would go to the trouble to pave a trench floor?

Stranger still, the dead men, clearly French judging by their uniforms, had a look of terror plastered on their faces. I approached one and examined the corpse.

A thick woolen coat obscured most of the body, but the forearms were outstretched with the fingers splayed as if to ward off something. One of the legs was twisted at an inhuman angle, the soil around it stained in blood. The eyes and tongue were gone. Probably the result of rats as there was no bullet or bayonet wound.

What could have killed him?

His rifle lay half-sunken in the muck next to his corpse. I wandered over to another body. More of the same. Too late in the game to see if either of them got off a shot, or even how old the corpses were. In fact, they looked almost mummified. In this damp weather, I would have assumed they would be rotten. I was too numb and tired to feel truly frightened, but a nagging sense of horror creeped in.

The channel twisted around and then abruptly ended at a wall of dirt.

This was it? Shouldn't there be a link to a reserve line or something?

I walked over and inspected the side of the wall. Nothing unusual. Loose, soggy dirt, with a root or two straggling out. I turned and examined the right side. Again, nothing unusual. Except that the dirt looked a bit firmer. I almost left it alone, but there was something unsettling about it.

Unshouldering my rifle, I stabbed at the wall with my bayonet. The tip sank into something solid, and I pulled back, but the bayonet was stuck. Withdrawing my knife, I dug around the buried bayonet.

Apparently, it was stuck in a buried slab of wood. Some sort of crude door by the look of it. A cleft around the blade opened into a dark aperture beyond. Bracing my palm again the muddy wood, I yanked fiercely. My feet started to slip, and I had to gyrate like a contortionist just to keep from falling. The moment I'd gained some stability, my bayonet broke free, and I almost fell back. My pack threatened to spoil any chances I had, the weight pulling at odd angles as I twisted about. My muscles ached, and a stinging sensation in my inner thigh told me I had probably pulled something, but I managed to regain my balance. Catching my breath, the straps of my pack dug into my shoulders. I drew in closer to the cleft in the wall. It was too dark to see inside, but a slight rush of cool air mixed with what I recognized as the scent of the sea drifted from it.

Was I that close to the coast?

Delving my fingers around the edge, I pulled forward, trying not to move too much and risk slipping. The buried chunk of wood shifted gradually, the last vestiges of mud grudgingly holding it back. Suddenly, it gave up the ghost, erupting in a dramatic spray of dirt. As the dust cleared, a short tunnel, maybe five feet tall, spread out before me. At the end of it a row of stone steps descended into a dark void.

What the fuck was this?

I stepped back and glanced at the trench. The sun had risen higher in the sky, and the dank floor had heated up, emitting a foul odor. The wind was whipping overhead and rustling the barbed wire. Then I heard voices.

Were those some of my missing unit?

I couldn't make out what they were saying. Many of the German infantrymen had a sort of live and let live philosophy toward isolated soldiers, but all that might have changed with the offensive. I could be behind enemy lines. The voices drew closer. They didn't sound German—more like some weird dialect that I couldn't make out. As I eased into the hole, I noticed that the phrasing had a weird, slurring quality. A strange apprehension gripped me. Something in my head screamed.

Run!

Half-stumbling, half-falling, I flew down the steps.

OUT OF THE FRYING PAN AND INTO THE...

My heart thumped in my chest, my armpits grew wet and sweat streamed down my forehead. The steps I was on twisted down in a loose spiral. A pale glow started to emanate from the depths and the arcing walls began to remind me of the catacombs I'd seen in books. The voices above receded further as I made yet another turn, and the path leveled out into a damp, cobblestone road, water crossing in glimmering stretches of black. Small creatures swam in depths, churning the water into a milky haze.

The walkway trailed a few feet before opening into a larger cavern. Stalagmites stretched from floor to ceiling. A soft rustling descended and glancing up, I saw a myriad of tiny pinpricks of light.

Bats.

I slowed my progress as I neared a larger chamber. A glow was coming from inside, and the walkway narrowed as it approached. Once I reached the edge my mouth fell open.

Each side of the room harbored five man-size glass tubes. The tops were capped in black, a twisting mass of cables sprouting atop. Even stranger still, each tube harbored a body that was floating in a greenish liquid and assailed by a steady stream of rising bubbles. All were naked young men and they appeared to be asleep. Corrugated black tubes emerged from deep within their throats.

I slowly approached the closest one. Near the base, on a small, curved placard accompanied by weird, hieroglyphic-looking forms were the letters-

"Himmler, H."

I wandered over to the next one. A soiled smear obscured the last letter, but I could make out the word "Goebbels."

I examined the next one-

"Hitler, A."

What is this?

I heard a low hiss and dived behind one of the tubes. My pack caught, and as I tried to unbuckle it, rocky slabs stabbed into my back. I almost cried out but managed to muffle my groans as I crawled behind the cylinder. The click of boot heels drew closer, and I scrunched down, peering around the edge. And what I saw...was horror...

The uniforms were German, but their occupants defied description. Spiky helmets only partially obscured a beady row of eyes, the skin contorting over a series of bony ridges. The shoulders of the uniforms struggled with sharp, inhuman edges. The hands were a writhing mass of tentacles. I sank back slowly, and my mind reeled.

Was I still asleep?

I heard a hiss, and before I could turn around something sharp pricked the base of my neck.

My dreams were terrible things. I spiraled down, alighting in a land of monsters. A man with a tiny mustache was spewing angry streams of what sounded like German. Foam coalescing at the corners of his mouth, hordes of people were raising their hands and shouting back.

The scene folded into another, and now I saw giant mechanical creatures on the sloping hills of France. Men road them and the trunks spit fire. I screwed my eyes tight and clutched my head, trying to wake up.

As I opened my eyes, I was on a desolate hill. It was night and I saw the forms of men in trench coats shuffling about. Shiny silver skulls glistened on their lapels. An old man with a long, straggly beard was telling them something. He was wearing strange, coarse garb and his eyes glittered with madness. Everything faded again, and then I was on an ancient cobblestone road, wandering into some distant town. Beautifully constructed buildings rose all around me. People in the distance were gathering on a sidewalk to talk. They were well dressed, and looked friendly, but I couldn't make out what they were saying. It sounded German. I heard a buzzing overhead and looked up. The sky darkened in a flock of silhouettes. Suddenly fire broke out all around me. People were screaming, buildings were disintegrating. A thin blonde girl, her dress consumed in flames, burst out a fiery doorway, her mouth a cacophony of screams.

Tears started streaming down my cheeks as the scene before me blurred. Some new horror awaited me, and I feared I would never wake again.

THE BEAUTY OF

IGNORANCE

THE INNOCENCE OF YOUTH

When I was young, I never wanted to kill anything. I didn't want to be responsible for snuffing out a fiercely burning torch of possibilities. Now, I no longer care.

The tall wild grass is a crisply waving sea of yellow, the beady kernels mingling with floating motes of dust in an upward ascent towards oblivion. I glance skywards and notice long, shredded trains of clouds stretching across the sky. Serene. Placid. Utterly deserted. This is where I found the body.

It didn't even look human. The long, narrow skull was garnished with large, curved teeth, looking like a cross between a Neanderthal and a feral dog. It was half buried under a mire of waist-high grass and made the small hairs on my spine stand up. The burnt smell of autumn suddenly grew stagnant, the air now tainted with decay. I strained my ears as I remembered every horror movie I had ever seen. Swiveling my head slowly, I fully expected to encounter something awful.

But there was nothing.

Sweat trickled down my forehead, and I ran. My lungs burned, and my legs, despite my best efforts, felt like they were moving in slow motion. I bounded over swarming nests of roots, hurdled a rotting trunk, and stumbled through a fallow trench, finally delving into the cool shade of the forest. Pausing, I stopped to catch my breath as my head swiveled madly about. Pines dotted the woods, masses of vines drooping down in tangled masses. I started back up and pushed forward, skipping over rocks and underbrush. My feet tripped through the dried carcass of a giant mushroom, the stagnant powder exploding about me.

Gasping for air, I tore at my face, desperately wiping away the blinding detritus.

As I kept running the trunks multiplied, the forest darkened, and I descended into the blackened heart.

BURIED IN THE FOREST

I didn't know where I was. The flowing landscape of oak leaves and pine needles spread out in a never-ending carpet. It broke out into leafy meadows before the forest swarmed back in and tramped through a labyrinth of similar-looking trees. Leaves whistled in their spiraling descent, small animals rustled in the underbrush, and all signs of civilization were far at hand. No automobiles, no machinery and no discourse. I kept running.

An hour later I stumbled out into an overgrown pasture. A farmhouse rose in the distance. The red sides were faded with neglect, dark splotches of wood visible through patches of peeling paint.

I slowed as I approached, my eyes fixed on the ancient-looking white door, its veneer broken by a single small window. The grass parted into a dirt path as I drew near the porch, and I ascended a rickety staircase onto a buckled front terrace. Damp timber assaulted my nostrils with its stink of rot and decay. As I drew in, I pressed my ear against the door. Nothing. I glanced around. The lawn stretched through an unkempt meadow and toward a far-off tree line. Dark purple clouds rolled by overhead, urging the afternoon into an early night. The house terrified me, but not as much as returning to the woods.

I tried the door. Unlocked. Pushing it open, I slowly entered.

PAST THE PORTAL

Dark and musty, faint daylight broke through velvet curtains to reveal poorly tended hardwood planks. An antique couch confronted me, its cherry wood arms curled up into elegant spirals. A low glass table stretched out before it, the remnants of a yellowing paper splayed across the top. The air smelled of fermented spices and slow decay.

As I ventured inside, my feet squished through something organic. Peering down, I tried to see what I'd stepped in, but the lighting was too poor. I could only make out that it was bubbly and dark. A faint scent of iron wafted past and a low groan pierced the air. The skin on my face tightened, and I stood as still as I could manage. Another groan, followed by a creak, and a body rolled off the couch. Hitting the floor with a heavy wallop, the collision resounded thunderously in the silence.

"Mister?"

My voice sounded tiny, choked by the lump in my throat.

"Ugh... fucking snot-nosed kid... you're trespassing..."

Sweat trickled down my face. I wanted to turn and run, but curiosity getting the better of me, I inched forward. A grizzled old man glared at me from his perch on the floor, a thin stream of drool dribbling down his stubbly chin. A soiled finger pointed accusingly at me as I noticed he was missing half of his right leg, loose strips of gauze trailing from the bloody stump. The smell of oxide and a wave of nausea struck me simultaneously.

"What happened to you..."

"Fucking punk kid, I told you to get out of here!"

There was now an edge of panic in his voice. Whatever did this was probably out there, maybe in those woods, and there was no way I was going back out in the dark!

"I can't... I'll... something... bad..."

He coughed, a spray of spittle flying out.

"You have no idea... no idea..."

He hacked again and rolled sideways. I didn't move. For quite a while. The room grew steadily dimmer, as lightning crackled and it began to rain.

The heavy breathing had stopped, replaced by a thin, lowly wheeze. I circled around the coffee table, delicately to avoid waking the old man. Just beyond him was a staircase, the steps ascending into darkness. I glanced around. A moldy smell wafted out of the kitchen, the crusty tips of unwashed pots and pans glistening in the pale light. The black maw of the upstairs held an intimidating unknown, but higher ground seemed safer than remaining here.

The stairs ended up being much steeper than they appeared, twisting and winding as they ascended. Darkness closed in even more, the padding of my feet the only assurance I was on solid footing. I grew disoriented, the environs melding into a hazy, dreamlike tunnel. A weird, electric tickle started to build up as a moist thickness filled the air. The bitter scent of metal accompanying it.

I spiraled around one last curve and saw a gleaming line above. It appeared to be the under-lighting from a closed door, and I thought about heading back down the steps. But that creepy old man seemed more daunting than whatever was beyond that door.

THE ROOM

The door was unlocked, the lever clicking wearily as it turned. When I pushed the door open, I was bathed in pale blue light. A thick fog roiled around me. A humming kicked in and quickly rose into a painful pitch as I wandered into the fog. My sight warped as blurry strings of white shot into the corners of my vision. Falling to my knees, the noise buffeted me in waves. Goosebumps sprang up on my arms, the sheen of sweat coating my face growing cold.

After a few minutes, the fog cleared a bit, and I could make out a pair of eyes watching me. They were cold and reptilian, with long, slime coated teeth beneath. That's when reality failed me.

SOMEWHERE FAR FROM HOME

I started, uncurling into a bright, sunlit vista. A cold, sharp wind cut through my jeans, making a mockery of my hoodie. As I coiled my arms, I slowly rose.

I was on a small, sandy patch, the tips of buried rocks surrounding me. A few feet in front, a sheer cliff dropped down into a misty abyss. Bending my head back, I watched as streams of gray clouds tumbled overhead, obscuring a dull sun. A thin trail descended through the bluffs behind me and seeing nothing else, I started towards it.

Down and down it went, an endless trench of sand between impossibly high walls of granite. Wind whistled fiercely above, with the theatrics of a living thing, but did not invade my small tunnel. Fossils were occasionally imbedded in the walls, only the creatures imprinted on them were hideous, resembling nothing I had ever seen before. I shivered and kept walking. The pathway finally widened, spreading out into a broad, flat plateau of wispy bushes and bleached sand. The wind was stronger here, whipping around the mountainside and dispatching spurts of debris. As I stumbled forward, the short plateau fell away into a jagged drop.

Narrow valleys below curved through a rolling mist, their contours fading in and out of view amidst the drifting smog. The hills were marred in dark clusters. With a closer look I noticed that they appeared to be huts.

Somehow I knew these huts!

Not them exactly, but what they represented. They were the complete antithesis of anything related to man.

I don't even know how I knew that.

My perception of reality drew in upon itself once again, and I stumbled back. A hallucination of prehistoric man, naked and filthy, wormed itself into my brain. Tears streamed down his soiled face as a child, probably his, screamed bloody murder as its limbs were hacked off.

ONE STEP FORWARD, TWO STEPS BACK

I awoke in the cabin attic, the cold light of dawn slicing through a cobweb-glossed window. Gathering myself up from a sprawl I looked around. Stacks of old magazines fought for space amidst weathered cardboard boxes. The middle of the floor harbored a familiar trapdoor.

I scrambled to my feet, my bones crackling like those of an old man. Pulling on the loop, throwing my back into it when it didn't budge, the door slowly opened. The wood was much heavier than I remembered, but opened on steps that descended into what I think was the cabin.

What had I just seen?

The image was fading already, like a dream you awaken from, convinced it was real, only to have it fade from your memory. I was terrified of whatever awaited me below, but after about two minutes that felt more like ten, I put on a stiff upper lip, held my breath, and started down.

The light dropped away as I descended, the wood creaking loudly under my feet. After what seemed an eternity, the stairs ended with a closed door, visible only by the slivers of light that outlined it. I pushed on it. Nothing. I ran my hands up and down, feeling for a handle. Nothing. I pounded on it. Still nothing. I dropped to my knees, curled my fingers under the doorframe, and pulled. There was a groan, and the door started to ascend. Then it switched course and started to drop, almost crushing my fingers. I jerked up, shaking my hands. A slight wedge was still open, and I slipped my fingers under and pulled. The door flew upwards with a sudden urgency.

A dusty hallway stretched out before me. Planks of cherry wood, their smooth contours buckled with age, adorned the walls. I ventured in slowly, the hardwood floor creaking underfoot.

The hall ended at a giant oak door. Turning the handle, I entered the shadows of a familiar room. It was the living room I had first encountered. The old man was missing, the bare couch stained in dark splotches. The bright light of early morning poured through the veiled window, cutting a shaft of brilliance across the coffee table. A yellowing newspaper, dated 1908, rested atop.

"Still here, huh?"

I swiveled my head. The old man reclined in a nearby chair, genteelly sipping out of a glass flask on some amber fluid.

"*What...*"

Flustered, I glanced down at his stump of a leg, now neatly bandaged, a new set of pants rolled up just above the wound.

"*Heh... You don't want to know...*"

His words were slightly slurred. He was half-drunk, but his beady eyes gleamed with wit, and a biting knowledge of something far deeper.

"*There are things that far pre-date man... things not so much dead as... displaced... Heh.*"

He seemed to amuse himself with that description and took another swig.

"*I've lived...*"

A hacking cough cut him off.

"*Way too long. There is no good to come of it. They only take. You think you have the upper hand... but they only take...*"

I looked down at his leg.

"*This?*"

He gestured at his missing appendage.

"This I deserved. Asked for, really. I was tempting fate. It's just a small token, all things considered."

He broke into another fit, a cross between coughing and muffled laughter. I glanced at the front door. It was slightly ajar, and I darted for it. Bursting out into the sunlight, I broke out into a mad dash.

Tall weeds whipped at my chest. I sucked in air like it was the most precious thing on earth, and even in my mad scramble, tripping through the ravines and underbrush, I managed to keep from falling. The thick smell of soil and grass closed in. My nose ran, my heart beat like a racehorse, and every hair on my body was standing on end. But I made it back into the woods.

I ran a good mile, navigating through towering pillars of bark. The dried remnants of fallen leaves and twigs violently snapped beneath my feet, and small groves of underbrush suffered my full assault as I plunged madly through. Finally, I stumbled out into the meadow I had come across much earlier. I slowed for a moment, my head throbbing. Blood rushed to my face as I rested my hands on my knees. Sweat poured down my forehead, tasting salty as it hit my lips. Then I heard a rustling in the grass and I took off again.

I couldn't feel my legs, and didn't realize how incredibly tired I was, until I broke out into my sun-dappled backyard. The forest behind me now held a barely fathomable terror. Getting to my house entailed scaling a steep hill, but that elevation provided me with some relief, some barrier from the woods. My thighs burned, my feet felt far too short, but I stormed up.

CURIOSITY KILLED THE CAT

'm stupid, I know. I couldn't avoid going back. I waited months, and then spent half my Saturday exploring the woods, telling myself I wasn't really headed to that old house, all the while steadily inching closer.

It looked even more decrepit in the bright light of afternoon, yet no less terrifying. As I approached, navigating my way through weeds that almost topped my head, I noticed the old man was out front. He was reclining in a rocker, under the shade of the sagging awning, and looked even older in the light of day. I glanced at his leg. Dark corduroy trousers ended in white socks and a black leather shoe. I looked over at the other leg. Same thing. Had I imagined it?

"*Oh no, boy, it's all quite real. Heh.*"

"*I... don't know... I mean...*"

I could swear he tried to laugh, but instead broke out in a hacking cough.

"*It let you live. And if it let you live, that must mean it somehow favors you.*"

"*But I... What let me live?*"

The corners of his face curled up into a slight grin. It was the most terrifying thing I had ever seen.

"*Come with me, I want to show you something.*"

He rose to his feet. A slow affair that was accomplished by no small amount of effort, and as he shuffled towards the door, he waved for me to follow. I paused, staring up at him. I had a feeling that my whole world was about to change. And as it turned out, I was right.

THE BITTERNESS OF AGE

We don't all die slowly. Some of us don't die at all, we just wish we did.

The wind tugs at the open collar of my leather jacket, and I bury my hands in my pockets. Almost nightfall. The sky is still not completely dark, decorated at its lower echelons by streams of orange and purple. I draw in a deep breath and am assailed by the smell of burning hickory, the ever-present scent of fall. A curled leaf, its limbs twisted and mangled in the throes of death, collides with my arm. Its wind-borne glide cut short; it falls away into obscurity.

I haven't been here in twenty years, but it feels like coming home. A turbulent, dangerous homecoming, but a homecoming nonetheless.

I miss my wife. I thought we would grow old together. We shared so much. Moves, career changes, even car accidents. The trials and tribulations that make up the bumpy tide of life. I never wanted anyone else after I met her. I graduated from boyhood to manhood in her company. I can still see her smiling face, drawn up in a slight look of sarcasm and playfulness. So talented. So beautiful. And such a waste. She would still be alive if it weren't for small minds and stupid people. Stupid, evil people. But they have no idea. No idea what they have done. They took from me the one thing I truly treasured.

The woods are a strange and evil place, bespeaking horrors that lie just beyond. Waiting, lurking in the shadowy recesses. Waiting to be invited into this world. The old man—and he is much older than he first appeared—had found things. Inhuman things, mumbled about only in legends. A world traveler, he had come across a city in the middle of nowhere, its massive pyramid constructed of perfectly carved blocks. Unnaturally perfect. Camping out, he had excavated for days. Eventually stumbling across a discovery so horrific he would only tell me about in small tidbits. All this in the elusive search for a fountain of youth.

And it existed, in a way, but it was too late. He had grown old and bitter, abandoning a centuries old home in the Scottish countryside for the isolation of colonial New York. Time had passed, but he had not. Whatever he was in contact with both tormented him and endowed him with enormous favors. Even a glimpse was fascinating, but I knew, deep down, that I had to get out while I still could.

It ended rather abruptly, my family moved and in time I tried to forget. It was almost fortunate, like I had been given an easy out. You do incredibly stupid things in the ignorance of youth, and as I grew a little older, I felt increasingly lucky. But that's all over now. I have nothing left to live for, and I desperately crave revenge. To the point that it's all I think about. Day and night. I thought that obsessiveness, that complete nihilism, was the stuff of movies. Taxi Driver. Falling Down. That sort of thing. But when it happens to you, your whole perception changes. Something was taken from me. Something I will never recover from. It's a lie, nothing ever gets better with age.

NO GOING BACK

After passing through a mottled curtain of tree trunks I saw that the man was still there. Both him and his house, looking not a day older than when I first encountered them twenty-five years ago. Which isn't saying much since they both looked decrepit then. He was in a chair on the porch again, sipping on a cup of something hot. The steam rose in thin, pirouetting streams that stroked his whiskers.

"*So, you've come back.*"

"*Yes.*"

"*You want something, I can tell.*"

"*Yes. My wife. She's dead...*"

"*I know this.*"

"*You do? But-*"

"*You never really leave. You had your chance, and you blew it. But you know all this. I told you years ago. What is it you've come back for?*"

"*I want someone dead.*"

The creases around his eyes tightened. His face registered no emotion, but I could swear he was laughing.

"*You know what this means?*"

"*Yes.*"

"*Once this is done, once this is unleashed, there is no going back. You must hate this person very much.*"

"*People. And yes, I do.*"

"*Well, it was mainly one person. Revenge doesn't bring her back.*"

"I know this. You're wasting my time. Are you going to help me or not?"

He chuckles. A deep, throaty laugh that leaves no doubt it is at my expense.

"Still a snot-nosed brat, I see."

His look grows more solemn, and he slowly rises.

"Follow me then."

THE BITTERSWEET TASTE OF IT

A man, sequestered in a small efficiency in Brooklyn, springs out of his sleep, sweat soaking the white sheets that entangle him. Greasy rivulets run down his face, splintering into tiny beads of fear as they break over black stubble. Squat and muscular, he tosses the sheets aside, rising naked in the darkness, ready to deal with whatever is tormenting him. He hears chatter, a liquid coiling, and reaches for the 9mm in his bedside drawer. That's when he loses his hand. Blood spurting like a fountain, he screams like a little girl. Long, slender teeth, the needle-sharp edges streaming tendrils of slime, is almost the last thing he sees. Almost, but not quite. It gets worse. His cries wake the neighbors. In a borough skeptical of the police, they kick in the door. Blood coats the room from floor to ceiling. Clusters of gore lie strewn about in mounds of glistening white and red.

And that is only the beginning. He has a family. Girlfriends. Accomplices. Not everyone is guilty, at least not of the crime at hand, but it makes no difference. No difference at all.

CHRISTMASS IS CANCELLED

THE NORTH POLE

Life is almost inhospitable. Dark and dreary, a blinding wintry mix obscures the sunlight, transforming the land into a dimly lit world of stinging particles and breathtaking cold.

But Santa doesn't mind so much. Hunching his huge frame against the weather, he wanders out of his cozy den and into the blanketing turbulence. Knee-deep in snow, he trudges toward the shadowy stable harboring his reindeer. Whistling to himself, his half-open red coat flapping in the wind, he thinks only of the coming holiday. His once-a-year trip around the world. He's been doing it for centuries, for as long as he can remember. He has always obeyed.

The horses neigh and stir, more out of anticipation for their approaching master than any discomfort. They were bred for the cold, just like Santa, and it doesn't bother them so much either. A hollow of darkness, the stable is illuminated only by the pale lines of sunlight cast by the door frame and a few slivers that pour through the cracks in the walls. The door edges open, ushering in a cascade of airborne snow. With a jolly cackle, a slightly inebriated Santa steps inside. He makes the rounds, gently petting submissive heads, mumbling unintelligibly about mission, duty, and some other bullshit. It's beyond their comprehension, but they appreciate the affection, and respond with gentle nudges and hoarse breathing. After a few minutes, Santa, apparently done with the drunken pep session, departs, leaving the door ajar as he stumbles toward the buried entrance of his abode.

His dwelling tunnels deep into the rock, widening into a large, oval cavern far below. Pausing at the doorway, he glances at the blizzard-obscured recesses on his left. Out there, hidden in the storm, are the barracks of the elves. He couldn't do it without them. They awaken every year, filing out of their cocoons, and proceeding to spend the next several months crafting toys, repairing the sleigh, and getting everything ready for the glorious night of December twenty-fourth.

He smiles, reminiscing the way Christmas used to be, in much more violent times. Then he throws open the door and wanders inside.

SUCH A NICE NIGHT

The wind whips past, the clouds a labyrinth of hills and troughs below the airborne chariot. A bright moon illuminates the crests of a million small opaque mountaintops, all undulating in a hazy sprawl as far as the eye can see. Maybe he'll get some of those nice folks, the kind that leave him spiked eggnog. He smiles, his thick lips peeling back to reveal a row of horse-like teeth.

An hour passes, and the mist grows thicker. Icy particles pelt his face, and visibility diminishes. He gently coos to the reindeer, and wriggles the reins, calming them and keeping them in line. The sleigh hits a pocket of warm air and rises abruptly, falling again just as it starts to ascend. The reindeers neigh in dismay, but he keeps up the gentle, reassuring sounds, increasing his grip on the leather straps. Suddenly, a rearward gust pushes him forward, and the top of his cap flops in front of his eyes. The carriage jolts harshly, and he can feel the reigns twisting in his hands. Desperately pushing back the brim of his cap, he throws a glance at the spot where the clouds have brightened into a red glow.

No, not one glow, several glows.

The gale was whipping by incredibly fast, darkened thunderheads roiling in front of the lights and obscuring their presence. Abruptly, the lights speed toward him, then just as quickly back off and dart away. The reindeer are spooked and start to break their forward stride. Everything became chaos for a moment as the animals all charge in opposite directions, quickly followed by the sound of rending leather.

For the first time, panic hits Santa. There is a brief moment, as if before a car wreck, when everything slows down. A cry of dismay... hands gesturing wildly... then suddenly, he is falling. The clouds that seemed so solid moments before revealing their true composition as he sails through them. He opens his mouth, but no sound comes out. He twists around, and a wide expanse of forest below is racing towards him. He tries to turn, to gain some form or composure, but it was like turning in the water, everything was too slow. Then he slammed into something and everything went black.

The Great Outdoors

A cough, a crystallizing reality, and Santa rolls over, spitting up melted snow. Every part of his body aches, and he can feel the breeze tearing through the holes in his clothing. He sputters specks of crimson across the snow. Groaning, he struggles into an upright squat, his eyesight still blurry.

Darkened shadows move listlessly before him, and he throws up his hands to ward them off. With a subdued neigh, a tongue licks the side of his face. Startled, he pulls away. The thing moves closer and licks him again. It's one of his reindeer! He reaches out and gently strokes the head. A contented murmur, and the creature sways gently, acknowledging the affection.

Santa tries to rise, nearly making it to his feet, then stumbles back. Cursing, he tries to rise again. His legs ache, a stinging sensation shoots up his right side, but he manages to struggle over to the leaning trunk of a massive tree. He can feel the hard bark pressing through the tear in his jacket, but he leans farther in, trying to take some of the pressure off his leg. Hot and throbbing, he must have twisted an ankle in the fall. Raising his head, he pulls back his cap. His vision has started to clear, and he blearily surveys the landscape.

Tall trees encircled him, their branches bedecked with a crust of snow. He returns his attention to the reindeer. Huddling about in a mass of bewilderment, their skinny legs are buried knee-deep in snow. A couple of them have lowered their heads and poked at something, sniffling loudly in disapproval.

Santa sloshes over, struggling through a thick morass of icy snow. The animals draw back, stumbling awkwardly through the deep drifts. All except one, which seems intent on investigating something. As he draws closer, it becomes apparent that one of the reindeer didn't make it. Leather straps entangle it's lower reaches, the upper thighbones breaking through the skin.

Fuck.

Prancer. One of his favorites. A lone tear rolls down his cheek, and his beefy shoulders sag. With a violent snort, Prancer's resting head comes alive. As the rest of the reindeer back away, a spray of blood flies out of its nose and splatters across the snow. It neighs madly, twisting its head back and forth in delirium. His sadness grows, and a tear runs out of Santa's other eye. His breath shallow, he leans over and grips the neck. Steadying his hands, he delivers a quick, ferocious twist. A loud pop, and the reindeer falls silent. Squeezing his eyes shut, tears run down his cheeks.

LOST IN THE WOODS

The woods flowed on endlessly. The sun was rising, enlivening the all-encompassing blanket of snow with a pale blue tint.

Two days passed, and Santa was starting to feel hunger. He ate more than a normal man, storing fat for his year-long slumber, and all this activity was maddening. His ankle had almost repaired itself, but that was burning calories he couldn't spare. If he could just find his sleigh, he could tie the reindeer to it, and off they would sail. His masters might be upset that he missed Christmas, but he hadn't seen them in eons, and surely they would understand.

He crested yet another hill and looked out over a valley. Bright and clear, it looked just like the last hill he had surmounted. An endless flow of trunks swarm over the land. A lazy tapestry of clouds roll overhead; their undersides tinged in a pale orange. The reindeer mill about, shuffling in nervous anticipation. Santa was starting to feel hopeless. Nothing was alive in this wintery landscape. No nuts or berries, no wildlife. Hell, even the trees were deep in hibernation. They had followed a vaguely circular route, heading out in wider and wider loops as they looked for the sleigh. If much more time passed, the reindeer would be too weak to attain flight, and all would be lost.

Santa had no idea what might happen after that. He had followed the same pattern for centuries, almost as far back as he could remember. His stomach burned with hunger, and he felt physically weak. Perhaps if he followed a straight trail back... not the long arc around but cutting right through where they had first landed. He was getting too far out now, and the sleigh probably wasn't here. He remembered it being with them much of the fall, a heavy load of presents pelting him as he fell. He had seen traces of them, small craters of snow festooned with hints of red and silver tinfoil. Surely the sleigh, being so much heavier, had not ventured too far. Surveying the reindeer huddled about him, all staring up with a glossy, fearful look in their eyes, he decided it was their best bet. Screwing up his eyes in determined resignation, he headed back down the hill.

AND WOULDN'T YOU KNOW

The trip back was relatively short, cutting directly through the snowy banks and into the darkened recesses of the woods. It was also a last-ditch effort, much of the initial hope had long since dissipated. Three days had passed. The snow Santa ate to keep him hydrated only made him hungrier, and his poor reindeer looked the worse for the wear. A few had tried scraping at the bark of trees, searching for nourishment there, but to no avail. Everything was frozen solid. Santa had lost his hat somewhere in the woods, and thick, ropy strings of white hair fluttered about his balding head. His skin had grown pale and was now a sickly faded green, the warmer peach tones long since chased away. Little dried reservoirs of spittle had built up at the corners of his mouth, one overflowing in a thin stream down his chin. It was now growing dark, and the reindeer were barely keeping up.

The sun had fallen as the woods opened into a familiar clearing. Santa didn't recognize it at first, the clutches of a hazy memory hardly perceptive. As he drew closer, foil-covered boxes littered the snow. In a few cases, shafts of splintered wood had rent brightly colored boxes, gouging out unlucky bits of stuffed animals and plastic toys. In one, a stolid shaft of wood held aloft a delicately painted, life-size child's head. Then Santa's vision turned, alighting on the partially frozen corpse of his dead reindeer. The head remained at the awkward angle Santa had twisted it into, the eyes wide and glassy. The gums had peeled back, revealing a row of wide teeth. Santa's stomach grumbled, and he bent slightly in pain. He felt weak, dizzy, and for a moment vertigo almost overtook him. But the hunger kept his eyes riveted on Prancer. That's when the unthinkable crossed his mind.

NOT SUCH A GOOD IDEA

He thought twice about it. More than twice. It would be like eating his friend. But his survival instincts were kicking in, initiating a genetic autopilot that turned off all emotion and reason. All that mattered was survival. One of Prancer's legs was bent, and he snapped it off with a sharp crack. The skin was frozen to the muscle, and he couldn't separate it. He shed his gloves, gripped the fur with his thick fingers, and pulled as hard as he could. With a dry, scraping sound, a tuft came free. A small tuft. This was going to take a while.

An hour later, he had eaten his fill. A cold, hard, repulsive mass had accumulated in his stomach, and he looked down with disgust at the remains of the poor beast. It looked even stranger with one leg missing. Dizziness overcame him, and he slowly laid back. The reindeer had grown more skittish and backed away. Santa didn't notice. The surroundings were growing dim, but the sky overhead appeared to be brighter than ever. Only the bellies of the clouds overhead shifted and moved, making Santa feel drunk. He didn't really feel drunk so much as off balance, like he was just falling into—or waking out of—a dream. His eyelids peeled back more, and small flecks of orange bespeckled his irises.

A sharp crack rang out, and Santa rose. With a momentous crash, the carcass of the sled fell from the branches, burying its front end in a drift. A few boxes still clung to the back, one finally taking a death plunge and skidding out across the snow.

It had been there all along! If only...

But Santa's vision was fading. The reindeer whinnied and stomped in place. Something was agitating them. But they were starving, and freezing, and Santa was all they had ever known.

JOY TO THE WORLD

The Henderson house was a rather plain-looking two-story dwelling, its whitewashed shell nestled snugly beneath the trees. It stood on a descent street in the military housing suburbs of Newburgh, New York. The streetlamps cast circles of

pale yellow every few feet, the air alive in a cascade of
white.

A dim light shown through the latticed downstairs windows. Timothy wistfully eyed the Christmas tree from the safety of the stairwell railing. Softly twinkling lights encircled the giant tree, weaving in and out of a myriad of hanging ornaments. Glistening red balls, miniature porcelain depictions of the baby Jesus in the manger, striped candy canes. A smothering conglomeration of competing decorations. The recesses under the tree were stuffed with an array of colorful presents, but he knew more were on the way. A haughty classmate, a grade above his 3rd year, had tried to convince him that Santa didn't exist. That it was really his parents who put all the presents under the tree. He knew that wasn't possible, and he was here tonight to prove it. He had even laid out the traditional eggnog and cookies. It had been over an hour, but he was far too excited to sleep. He jumped at every rustle. So far it had only been the wind, but he kept his ears peeled.

A muffled grating started to emanate, and he anxiously glanced from door to chimney to window, trying to isolate the source. The scraping grew stronger, drawing his attention to the chimney. His heart jumped in his chest, and he held his breath. With a heavy thump, something black emerged from the recesses of the fireplace. Slapping his hand over his mouth to keep from crying out he ducked back behind the cover of the upper staircase. Something skidded across the floor, followed by heavy footsteps. Bending forward again, he peered around the bend.

Looks like Santa alright!

A bright red coat, red trousers, and heavy black boots. The head was slightly bent over, the back turned to him, but Santa appeared to be missing his hat.

He stood up and dared to take a few steps.

"I knew you were real!"

Santa froze, then slowly turned around.

Bulging bloodshot eyes, the irises a glistening orange, locked on him. Yellowish-green drool trailed from his mouth, intermingling with the crimson stains garnishing his beard. Santa's mouth opened, and a deep, guttural groan emerged. Timothy's jaw dropped, he turned, and scampered up the stairs. Two at a time.

Slamming his door, he fidgeted with the lock. Fixing it in place, he flew over to the closet, hashing through shoes in search of his snowsuit and boots. There was the sound of a door opening, followed by his dad's shrill voice.

"Hey, what's going on... Who are... Aaaaaahhh..."

A sickening snap was followed by a thick gurgling.

"Oh my god! Pete! No... Stay back..."

A second, even more grisly crunch followed. Then... silence. Timothy pulled on his snowsuit. He dug his boots out and was pulling them on when he heard another scraping. Pausing, left boot half on, he tried to focus. It sounded wet and repetitive. He strained his hearing more. It continued, and a horrible thought gripped him.

That's the sound I make gnawing on a chicken wing!

Pulling the boot on, heart beating a million miles an hour, he headed for the window. Then he heard a door creak open, and the sleepy voice of his sister.

"Mom? Is that you?"

A piercing scream was followed by the sound of a door slamming. He held his breath. All was silent for a moment. Then the steady gnawing sound resumed.

She's safe. Wendy is as safe as she's going to be...

He was too terrified to head back. He just knew that thing could be right on the edge of his door, but... his sister...

I have to find help!

Setting the lamp on the floor slowly so as to not make any noise, he crawled up onto the desk, unlatched the window, and cracked it open. There was the sharp sound of breaking ice, and he froze, listening for that thing in the hallway. But all was silent.

Is it waiting for me? Had he heard the window?

A moment passed, and the gnawing resumed. He edged open the pane, a gust of freezing air swooping in.

The roof sloped down toward a tree. He crept out, edging across the shingles and reaching out for the thick branches. He had done this a million times, but never in the snow. And never in a situation like this. He held his breath and listened. The gnawing had stopped. Something scraped along the floor, and a new sound greeted his ears.

Twitching?

It sounded like...

Sniffing! That thing is at my door!

In a panic, he clambered up onto the windowsill and hurdled over. With a thump in the snow, his feet started to slide. He desperately grasped at the window ledge, his legs sweeping out from under him. His thick mittens barely held on, slipping from the window railing until he was only managing to hold on by his fingertips. A trickle of sweat rolled down the side of his face and plunged into the fur lining of his hood.

"*NNNNghhhhh...*"

A guttural cry, followed by a pounding on his door. Timothy could feel his gloves slowly sliding off the sill. If he freed one hand to get a firmer grip, the other would surely give. He glanced over at the tree.

Could I make it?

"*NNNNNghhhhh...*"

A splintering sound, and thick fingers pierced through the door. He scrunched up his eyes and peered hard into the depths of the room. Something in the hole glistened. Squinting and focusing on the cleft, he could make out a slight gleam...

That thing was staring!

Heart pounding, he lost his grip. Picking up speed as he slid, he flopped around desperately, craning his neck to stare down at the fast-approaching gutter.

There's no way... I'm going to miss it!

He started to throw his hands in the direction of the tree, but it was too late and over the edge he sailed.

THE FURY OF THE STORM

The thick padding of snow softened his landing. There was none of the jarring shock when he jumped in the summer, but he tumbled awkwardly this time. Desperation seized him, and he was back on his feet immediately, slogging through the waist-high snow. He moved as fast as he could, but it still seemed so slow. Craning his neck, he looked over his shoulder. Santa had made it to the window, and was staring down, his eyes focused on him like a hungry dog.

The downstairs door handle rustled, popped open, and his shrieking little sister came flying out. She had the foresight to put on her winter clothes and looked almost comical. Wearing a heavily padded pink bodysuit that sprouted bunny ears, her white mittens were outstretched like lobster claws. A thin layer of ice coated the steps and walkway, and Timothy was afraid she would slip. He rushed across the remaining field of snow, meeting her in the recently shoveled driveway. Grabbing her hand, he turned and headed toward the road.

Their feet kept slipping, almost bringing him to his knees, but they made it through. Only upon reaching the curb did Timothy dare to look back. His little sister stared up at him, then followed his line of sight to the doorway. The entrance was dark but partially hidden in the shadow was the lurking form of Santa. He didn't move, but his eyes were fixed on them. The blood pounded in Timothy's temples. He tightened his grip on his sister and they fled out onto the road.

The storm was blinding. Soft, powdery drifts gave way underfoot, the loose snow slithering back in place as he tore through. Big, thick flakes fell from the sky, casting the streetlight in dotted queues of white. The wind picked up, biting his exposed face. He leaned his head into it and dragged his sister. They shuffled past the streetlight, over the curb, and into the neighbor's yard. The large, latticed window of the living room lay just beyond. Only the Christmas tree was aglow, its hundreds of little lights twinkling.

"C'mon..."

He was practically dragging Wendy. The drifts reached the middle of her chest and her face was scrunched in a mixture of anxiety and pain.

"We have to go... faster..."

"I'm trying... I'm trying..."

Across the lawn and up the snow-capped stairs they ran, Timmy finally letting go of his sister's hand to bang heartily on the door. His mittens muffled the sound, the wind drowning out all but the faintest thump. Pulling his hand out of the mitt, he rapped against the door, the cold making his skin thin and brittle. The door was heavy mahogany and responded to each blow with a sharp stab of pain.

"Help... help... somebody... please..."

The only answer was the wind. He pounded again, his knuckles growing raw. Nothing. With a desperate glance over his shoulder, he grabbed his sister's hand. He bounded off the steps, rounded the side, and headed for the sliding door in the back. His sister was waning, falling behind as her little legs wore down. But he couldn't carry her, at least not very far.

Damnit!

He paused, letting go of her wrist. Breaths erupted in sharp bursts and sweat started to pool in his armpits. His sister stared up at him, her pink hood and bunny ears eerily swaddling her terrified face. Her eyes were big brown globes, her cheeks blanched pink, but she issued not a sound. Just stared in uncomprehending alarm. He strained his ears, but the wind drowned out everything. Gripping his sister's wrist, he started back toward the rear of the house.

A drift had piled up against the sliding glass door, and he had to kick some of it free to reach the handles. Obscured by frost, the interior was dark and unviewable. The wide metal handle was just below his chest, and he pulled with all his strength. It didn't budge. Edging closer to the glass, he tried to put his weight against it as he pushed forward. His mittens slipped around the L-shaped handle, and he flew face first into the snow. Jumping up with a furious sputter, the melting crystals streaming in a freezing cascade down his neck, panic started to set in. He bounded over to the door, pulled his other mitten off, the cold wind flaying his cracked skin, and gripped the door handle. It was like ice, the metal biting into his palms. Tears welling up, he pushed forward as his rubber boots slipped backwards. Panting clouds of vapor, freezing air coursing down his throat, he screwed his eyes tight and shoved. A loud crack, and the seal of ice broke. Timothy yelped in pain, skin pulling free from his palms. He lost his balance and tumbled into the show again, his raw hands burying themselves in a waiting drift.

"Damnit. Damnit. Damnit...."

The curses were mouthed silently, Timothy rocking to and fro, tears streaming down his cheeks. His vision was blurred, but it was clear enough that he could see his sister standing over him.

"Timmy... we have to go...."

He grew insanely angry for a moment, but quickly calmed. It sounded so innocent. So childlike. But so true. He struggled to his knees, grabbed his sister's hand, and headed for the door.

BUT ALL THAT GLITTERS AS GOLD...

The silhouette of a couch, a large-screen TV just behind, were all that were visible. The thick shag carpet always retained a slightly fishy but spicy smell. Having released his sister to close the door, Timothy grabbed her again and headed toward the carpeted stairs. Holding his finger up to his mouth in the universal symbol for

Keep fucking quiet.

He took a stab at gingerly ascending the steps. It wasn't much use. His snow boots were like giant boats, and the stairs creaked with each step. Every issuance of noise caused him to tense, his ears stretching out in panic. It was nerve racking, but they had no choice—they couldn't stay below. His friend Daniel lived here, and his dad was a big guy. He was sure that if he got involved, things would be better.

Rounding a wood-paneled bend, they entered the wide living room. The Christmas tree was ablaze in a cascade of lights, a few foil wrapped presents encircling its base. A gilded armchair stood beside, accompanied by a marble-topped stool sporting a glass of milk and cookies. Timothy was sure that was for Santa, and not being touched meant he hadn't been here. Yet. But that was the old Santa. Maybe he wasn't interested in cookies and milk.

Maybe he never had been.

All the houses on the block were built the same. On the left-hand side there was a wooden balustrade. It escorted a flight of fourteen steps (he'd counted it many times) upstairs. His alcoholic grandmother had visited one year and passed out on the twelfth step. The two smaller rooms occupied by the children would lie across from each other, with the larger parental room just beyond. Holding his finger to his lips, he led his sister up the stairs.

The right-hand room was small, harboring a bed and dresser and nothing more. In Timothy's house, this was his sister's room, and he had been there many mornings. The two of them would stare out at the street, hoping the snowstorm would be intense enough to delay the plows, and more importantly, the school openings! They always grimaced when they saw the bulldozers.

The door was open. The small bed sheets were disturbed, but it was empty. In his house, his mom made the bed every morning, so he assumed it meant that Daniel's brother was recently there. The window was tightly closed, the sheet of snow on it casting a pale, creamy light over everything. Unless he was hiding in the closet, or under the bed, he wasn't in the room. Timothy was far too scared of either of those spots to check them out, so he ducked his head out and wandered over to the other room. The door was open, and this one harbored a bunk bed, probably for both when they were smaller, but now occupied only by Daniel.

"Daniel!"

It was a harsh, urgent whisper, and brought no response. This room was a little darker, and Timothy was even more hesitant to enter it.

"Daniel!"

It was louder this time, but there was still no response. The top of the wooden dresser sported a glass tumbler, and Timothy grabbed it. Tossing the contents over the top rail, a dull splash told him no one was there.

Damnit!

He still hadn't released the grip on his sister's hand, and as he swiveled back around, he pulled her toward the master bedroom.

The door to this room was only half open, and what lay beyond was completely impenetrable. He approached it more slowly, tiptoeing as he passed the doorframe.

"What's wrong?"

It wasn't that loud, yet the voice sounded like a bullhorn in the silence, and Timothy jerked his sister's hand, more out of instinct than anything else.

"Ow, you're hurting me!"

He spun his head around, shooting her a-

Shut your fucking mouth right now!

She stared back at him with a look that said-

I hate you and I'm going to tell mom.

He turned back to the room and peered in.

The bed was taller and wider than the ones in the kids' rooms, and whatever rested on it was hidden by the massive footboard. Creeping over to the right, he kept his eyes glued to the slowly emerging field of sheets. Just beyond, the bedspread rose into life-size lumps.

They were here! He was saved!

"Mister Havet?"

It was just above a whisper and brought no response.

"Mister Havet?"

This was louder, but still nothing. Tugging gently at the edge of the sheet, the thing was stuck. He yanked a little more, and it gave slightly. He paused, holding his breath.

That should have been enough to wake them!

A minute passed. Two. He gently reached over and pulled the sheet even harder. It still held, and he wrenched it harshly. The sheet came loose, a fusillade of crimson and black flying out and pelting him in gooey chunks. Blinded for a moment, when his vision cleared his jaw dropped. Rib bones jutted out of chunks of red, the slippery sheen of pink intestines worming their way through the exposed rifts and onto darkly stained sheets. The arm was gone, the face turned away. Chunks of gore poked up from the edges of a caved in skull. With a liquid sliding sound, the head rolled over, an eyeball tearing free and sliding down the cheek.

Timothy almost screamed. Almost... but his voice was gone, and in the few seconds it took to regain it, the sound was caught in his throat. Everything was silent for a moment, then he heard a liquid slurping sound, followed by a muffled crunch.

Oh shit! Oh shit!

Frozen, he couldn't move for a moment. Then he remembered his sister.

She hasn't screamed yet! That means...

And just then, an ear-piercing scream. The echoes of it were still resounding when he realized that the slurping sound had stopped. An enormous, dark figure rose on the other side of the bed.

It was Santa, mouth and chin coated in a flume of blood. A fingerless hand was held aloft, a piece of flesh still stuck in Santa's teeth. In horrific realization, Timothy noticed that the fingerless hand what that of a child. There was no time to think. He grabbed his sister and darted for the door. She yelped, twisting around gawkily, her little feet padding behind in desperation. They still couldn't keep up, and Timothy was nearly dislocating her wrist. Hitting the bottom of the steps, he scooped her up, twisting her on his back as he headed for the rear door.

ESCAPE INTO THE FOREST

Daniel's house was at the top of a hill, the backyard dropping in a steep slope that mellowed out before it hit the woods. They had sledded down it many times, the snow packed into channels of polished ice from their weekly adventures. Timothy looked around, trying to make out the contours of a sled in the blinding frenzy. The sun must have risen by now—the sky had lightened—but the fury of the storm obliterated any hint of daybreak. Even the edges of the house were barely visible, the walls assaulted by a furious barrage of white. Timothy glanced back at the rear door, and a renewed jolt of terror ran through. Grabbing his sister, he started down the hill.

The drop was fierce, his feet slipping a few inches with each new stride, but the thick barrier of snow kept him from going far. It was exhausting, and he didn't even feel tired so much, but more as if the energy in him was burning out. He tightened his grip on his sister, and she let out a clipped yelp in response. No time for niceties now, this was life or death.

The gale beat fiercely against his face, and he gritted his teeth as he tilted forward, the windborne flurry drumming his numb cheeks. As they hit the bottom, the progress became even harder. There was no sloping angle to work in their favor, just a never-ending mass of white that stretched out across the buried backyard. Timothy paused, drew his sister in close, and tried to catch a breath. He glanced back up the hill, it's steep incline obscuring the house. Just a blur crowned the top, flurries of snowflakes whipping in and out of focus. There was no sign of Santa. He readjusted his grip on his sister and started for the woods again. In the momentary break his legs had grown stiff, and they complained with the renewed strain, but he didn't dare stop now. If they could just get to woods, they might have a chance.

He had released his sister's wrist, and spun around in fright, half-expecting Santa to be there. But Wendy was alone. Exhausted, terrified, and confused, but alone. He reached over and took her hand, helping her up and across a mound of snow.

The forest floor was much more manageable, the snow only a few inches high. Timothy and Wendy trudged on in silence, a steady queue of condensed steam escaping their gasping mouths. The woods opened up into a field. Timothy thought about going around it, but the corner of his vision caught the depression of a trail. It wasn't much more than a depressed grove, but the path looked recent enough that the snow was not that high, and most likely it led to a highway. He let go of his sister's hand and stumbled forward, trying to get a better look. He didn't know the woods up here that well, but this field probably belonged to the same farmer that had chased him and his friend Dewey out last summer. He was a grumpy old man, threatening us with a shotgun. It was enough to make Timothy pause, but they had no choice.

"Wendy, we are going to cross this field. I think there is a highway on the other side."

She simply nodded. He grabbed her wrist and headed in.

The trail led them in a long, sweeping curve. The packed ground was treacherous, the going slow. The carpet of snow hid a plethora of shallow pools of black ice and both almost bit it more than once.

"Timmy... we have to stop... I'm tired..."

He was about to argue with her when he realized it would be easier to just let her catch her breath for a moment. He had no idea how far they had to go, but they had traveled a decent distance—and besides, there were no sounds of pursuit.

The neighborhood probably presented much easier pickings.

He shuddered at the thought, but all that mattered right now was getting to safety. He craned his head and looked up at the sky. The storm had abated slightly, and thick clouds roiled overhead. Timothy remembered the issue of *Creepy* he had been reading last night. There was a thing, an evil spirit, in the woods. People disappeared, only scraps of their bones were left. A fresh wave of terror gripped him, and he jolted upright. Beckoning his sister, he took note of the look of complaint on her face, yet she rose without a sound, and they started back down the path.

It wasn't that long before the trail rounded a bend, took a dive through a thicket of trees, and came to an end at the edge of a highway. The shoulder was buried under a mountain of blackened snow, apparently pushed off the road by the plows. It seemed the trail had been used since the last storm, as a break in the grimy slush tore through. Dragging his little sister behind, Timothy headed over.

Climbing up, Timothy stopped just at the edge of the road. Twin lanes twisted down in a long, sloping curve. On the other side was a cliff, the silhouettes of craggy mountains in the distance. Nothing else. Nothing at all. Just the wind. The soft rustle of snow-laden branches. The biting cold. Timothy had a sinking feeling.

CHRISTMAS IS CANCELED

They waited almost an hour. Timothy debated going out into the road and following it. They would freeze to death if they stayed out here much longer, but going back wasn't an option. That highway was dangerous. Two small kids, icy conditions, trucks moving at high speeds… they might be roadkill in no time.

He threw the choices back and forth, and decided they could risk another thirty minutes before they would need to move on. They would head toward the nearest place he knew—West Point. It wasn't close, around the mountain and miles away, and it took a good half an hour by car. In the summer.

A glimmer on the banks of snow caught Timothy's attention, and he looked up the road. An eighteen-wheeler was coming down the mountain, it's twin lights cutting through the mist. He started jumping up and down, screaming at the top of his lungs. The truck looked far away and separated by more than just distance.

It didn't look like it was taking any notice, its speed unchanged. Timothy peered around desperately. He grabbed a handful of filthy snow, crushed it into a snowball, and hurled it at the truck. It fell far short. He bent over and made a few more, popping up to hurl them at the truck, when he noticed that his sister had wandered out into the road!

"Nooooo..."

He screamed, dropping his snowballs, and running out after her. It was almost like she was in a daze, blindly shuffling forward, the truck looming more massive by the second.

Suddenly, there was the screech of brakes, the mammoth vehicle slowing to a halt as it abruptly angled for the side of the road. With a metal groan, the beast stopped, a series of hisses following in rapid succession. Wendy started to head toward it. Timothy bounded after her, almost slipping in the process. Just as he reached her, the door cracked open. A plump older-looking man, his face adorned by a straggly white beard, leaned out. He looked like something Timothy had seen in a Norman Rockwell painting. Then his voice broke out, sounding nothing at all like a Norman Rockwell character.

"What're you fuckin kids doin out here. Get killed in this shit!"

Crusty and soden, his words were practically spit out. He reminded Timothy of the gun-toting farmer.

"We... ah..."

He couldn't think of what to say. Anything would sound crazy.

"Please, our parents are hurt..."

"What're you doin in the middle a tha road? Get run over by a car. Don't you know how to work a phone?"

Timothy had to think of something. Had to convince him to take them to West Point. There were soldiers with guns there. That was his best chance.

"The phone's dead. Please. We need to make it to West Point"

"Fucking..."

And then he seemed to soften, like he wasn't so mean after all. Just cranky. He climbed down, picked up Wendy, and boosted her in. Timothy hurried over, flew past him, and scrambled up next to her. With a grunt, he hauled himself back up. The truck was still running, rumbling softly, and he pushed it into gear, heading back out onto the road.

"Put yer seatbelts on."

They snuggled next to each other, Timothy pulling the shoulder strap over them. It barely cleared their snowsuits and had to be forced into the receiver with no small amount of Timothy's fading strength. He needed a nap. Needed this bad dream to be over.

If only it was just that...

The truck picked up speed. The forest thinned on both sides as rocky cliffs of granite took over. Rounding a bend, the left dropped away into a forest far below, the road bordered by a thin metal rail. This had always terrified Timothy. He constantly imagined going over, the metal rail entirely inadequate to stop a speeding vehicle. Surely someone had fallen off. There had to be some wild stories. Harsh Buffalo winters, frozen roads...

This wasn't helping. He tried to concentrate on what to tell the people at West Point. And there was another question.

Who would he tell? What is even the main building! And it's Christmas! Will anyone even be there?

The only answer was the dull thunder of the tires, the swish of the wipers, and the constant pattering of the snow.

Minutes passed, although it seemed much longer than that, and they weren't even halfway there. Timothy had traveled this route with his dad many times, and it had always seemed much shorter. Only this time it was snowing. And the driver was drunk. Well, maybe not drunk, but definitely not sober. He just had to keep his mind occupied with something else.

Only ten more minutes. It always seemed longer when they started around the mountain, but it was never that long.

Suddenly, there was a loud thump, and blood splattered across the windshield. It was followed by the remnants of a half-eaten forearm, a ragged string of veins trailing behind.

"What the hell!"

The driver's eyes bulged, his hands jerking desperately at the wheel. Then everything happened in slow motion. The rear end started to fishtail. Timothy and Wendy were thrust forward, the strap of the seat belt the only thing holding them at bay. The mangled arm slid off the windshield, leaving behind a trail of gristle. Even through the screen of gore on the windshield, Timothy could see that they were now headed for the cliff. He opened his mouth to scream, but nothing came out. It was like a nightmare, one in which you wake up just before you hit the ground.

But if you died in a dream, you died in real life, too, right?

Timothy pinched himself, trying to wake up. The metal guardrail burst, the nose of the truck dived, and just as the view was panning down, there was a faint blur in the sky above.

Timothy could have sworn it was followed by a jolly-

"Ho Ho Ho..."

Only it was too carefree, too wild, and could have just been the wind. This didn't feel like a dream. Usually, at this point, everything was getting all incorporeal and weird. Then his sister started screaming, and it really didn't feel like a dream. The driver was blubbering something. All Timothy could think was that he didn't want to die. But that wasn't really up to him.

THE SMALL SPACES IN TIME

THE SKYSCRAPERS LOOK LIKE GRAVESTONES FROM HERE

And It Started So Nicely. Neatly polished bright white smiles and coiffed hair. Glistening. Corporate. Fake. The stewardess, her face transfixed in a perma-grin, welcomed me onto the plane. I smiled back. A cheeky, benign greeting that concealed the monster I was inside. Oh, and I was a monster. If she knew the real me, she would take her toothy façade and run, probably grabbing someone from Homeland Security as she passed. I glanced at her again. Shoulder-length brown hair, a navy-blue business dress, and that smile, which looked glued in place.

I peered down the aisle. A couple of the passengers were looking up, a cloudy hostility beating behind their weary eyes. It was my imagination again. I think. I proceeded down the row and took my seat, wrestling my neck pillow into place against the window. The cloudy vista outside was dark and soothing, and I was asleep before the stewardess embarked on her safety spiel.

My dreams were horrid. I'd lost something. Something significant. Something that I would regret losing forever. I think was a person. Maybe, enhanced by a place. A place I didn't live but could have. I tossed fitfully, and eventually woke in a panic. A lady snoozed beside me, her pale visage held together by a thick layer of makeup. Late thirties to early forties by the looks, the wrinkles just cracking out of the pancake of mascara she was wearing. I breathed in deeply and turned to the window. Wisps of cloud flowed over houses. Their hive-like structures were arranged in neat little patterns that marched across the landscape in a blind procession that declared what we all knew. That there were way too many people on this planet.

Bright blue circles contrasted with muted brown squares below. Swimming pools. Suburbs. The buildings started to crowd in together, losing their color and space as they grew in size and proximity. A population center. I wondered what city we were over and glanced at my watch. The second hand had broken off and was jamming the other two. It didn't matter. I could have pulled my cell phone from my bag, but I didn't really care. My eyes were already growing heavy again. I thought I'd sleep a little longer. Funny, the skyscrapers below looked like gravestones. No people, no mess. I drifted off.

RISE AND SHINE

I woke up abruptly.

How long had I been out?

The plane was bathed in an enveloping white light. I glanced to my left. Empty. The seats across the aisle were empty as well. I unfastened my seatbelt, scooped my bag out from under the seat, and rose to the highest crouch the curving roof would allow. All the seats were empty.

Did the plane land? Was I overlooked and left behind?

I crawled out into the aisle and straightened up. I pulled out my cell phone, but it was dead. Funny, I could have sworn I charged it. The far entrance was open, an intense light streaming in. Heading towards it, a creeping tension pounded away the last vestiges of my sleep.

At the door I looked out at the airport, its gate was contracted into a worn canvas accordion. There was no ramp of stairs leading from the plane. I tossed my bag to the ground below. Gripping the edges, I dangled by my fingertips and glanced around. The tarmac glistened to the point where it hurt my eyes. In the distance, a fueling truck and a few other vehicles were visible as sun-bleached silhouettes. Letting go, I dropped to the runway, my ankles protesting angrily as I hit. That stung more than I expected. Scooping up my bag, I ventured toward the nearest gate.

The whole airport was calm and quiet. Too quiet. As I neared the stairway, my sense of unease mounted. The shadows rolling underneath the stairs seem to have a mind of their own. I clamped my eyes shut, rubbed them, and stared again.

The intense light was blurring the edges, making me see things!

I reached the stairwell and slowly ascended. The door at the top opened into a shadowed interior, and I slowed down. Trudging up the worn carpet, the pathway eventually opened into a spread of empty halls.

Everything was on. The fluorescent overhead lights so intense they were gleaming off the polished tiles. The ubiquitous book/mini mart combo sprawled out just beyond, its shelves offering a colorful cornucopia of the latest magazines and best sellers. But there was no motion. And no people.

"Hello?"

I called out timidly, then again louder, a cracking desperation seeping into my voice.

"Hello? Anybody home?"

Staggering out into a glistening porcelain walkway, I came face to face with a large TV monitor that usually posted the arrivals and departures. But it was just a dark, featureless screen.

I heard something-a low moan-and almost jumped!

Glancing around, I called out again.

"Is someone there?"

Shambling forward, I swiveled my head anxiously as I passed the duty-free store with its carefully arranged pyramids of cigarettes and alcohol. As I passed I heard a soft slithering. Springing back and crashing into a shiny wall, I clawed my bag off and wheeled around. My skin had grown cold and clammy, the hairs on my back at full attention.

"Who's there?"

Nothing.

"I can hear you!"

Still nothing. A bead of sweat trickled down the side of my face. Scooping up my bag, I broke into a run.

As I tore down the hall, the sun hit me in strobes as I passed the gates. The pathway transitioned into an antiseptic sheen of fluorescence as I burrowed deeper into the bowels of the airport. A food court passed by all the restaurants well-lit and by all appearances open for business. But all were unattended.

I slowed, weaving through the tables as I approached the counter of a Chinese fast-food joint. Angled glass showcased neat metal bins; the trays carefully covered with stainless steel lids. Hurdling the counter, I ripped the lid off one. Empty. I ripped the lid off yet another. Still empty. Throwing the lid to the floor, it skipped away in a sharp rattle, and I heard a muted hissing noise. Jumping back over the counter, I stumbled backwards into the glare of the overhead lighting.

"Hello? Show yourself!"

Nothing.

I turned and fled back down the hall, shafts of light blinding me as I passed mammoth windows. My heart beat ferociously in my chest. My thighs burned and itched, and my calves cried out in fatigue.

I stumbled into the cookie cutter setup of an airport mini mart. Smashing into a shelf, magazines splurged out in a cascade of glossy pictographs. Twisting sideways, my knee banged painfully against unyielding particleboard, and I staggered back out into the hallway.

IT NEVER ENDS

It seemed like hours, although time has a way of distorting itself. This place was a labyrinth. Corridor after corridor offered up more of the same. Random airport shops, breaking open into food courts, then narrowing back down into shadowed corridors. Some were endowed with the grooved rubber and stubby glass walls of a moving walkway; some were not so fortunate. The motorized stretches of floor flowed by slowly, in a silent traipse toward oblivion. The stores and restaurants glowed with the cold, fluorescent glaze of apathy. I was tired. My legs ached. My feet were sore. I stumbled into one of the gates and plopped down on a crudely threaded blue chair. Sighing, I breathed in slowly, kicked off my vans, and stretched out. I was so sleepy. Nudging my bag in as a pillow, I was out the moment my head hit fabric.

A grating buzzing woke me, and I gasped as I sat bolt upright in the plane. The blond haired, young Martha Stewart lookalike next to me was staring quizzically. I must have been a sight! My mouth felt like it was full of cotton, and I could feel the I crusty tightness on the corner of my lip that told me I was drooling. Wide eyed, I swiveled my head. She smiled, revealing long, yellowed teeth. Too long.

"You know you're going to die in there?"

I started awake. I was in the airport. It had transitioned into night, the overhead lighting taking over for the drenching sunlight. Was that a dream... or is this the dream? I shook my head and stood up. This felt real... even more real than when I woke up in the plane. I picked up my bag and wandered out of the gate and back into the hallway. Sauntering aimlessly, I passed familiar landmarks. A Brookstone. A Starbucks. A McDonald's. All bright and sterile. And empty.

As I rounded a turn, I could make out a shadow occupying the farthest chair of the right-hand gate. My back hairs stood on end, my heart beat ferociously, and my eyelids peeled back. I froze in mid stride. Seconds passed, then minutes.

"Hey..."

I almost whispered it.

"Hey you..."

A little louder this time. I started shuffling forward, my pace picking up until it was a fast walk. As I closed in, the features resolved into that of a desiccated corpse. Shriveled and dry, its brownish skin wriggled in creased grooves from vacant eye sockets. The mouth had fallen open, it's row of lower teeth descending at an unnaturally sharp angle. It bespoke a degradation to the point where the tissue couldn't even hold the jaw upright. Wisps of hair flowed back in lifeless, sandy strands from a deflated scalp. A slate gray suit billowed in oversized folds over a skeletal body, the middle opening up on a sunken white dress shirt.

Shriveled fingers gripped the armrests. A little too tightly. It might have been natural decomposition, but the face looked strained—as if in a lot of pain at the moment of death.

I circled around behind, my attempt at keeping a several-foot distance a bit put upon by the proximity of the wall. The whole scene was dim and enshrouded in shadow, but as I drew behind, chills ran down my spine. The lower scalp hairs were matted with a dark substance, and there were three small punctures on the base of the skull. I leaned in for a closer look. Unmistakable. Deep holes.

What the fuck was this?

I really didn't want to touch the corpse, but I had to know. Slowly reaching out, I gave the head a poke. It moved. Something wasn't right. I gently reached in and cupped the head between my palms. It felt coarse and rubbery. I fought back a wave of nausea and jostled it slightly.

It was empty! Something had taken the brain!

I jerked back my hands and shook them violently. Holding them up, I could still see flakes of skin.

Fuck!

I scrubbed my hands madly on my jeans and held them up again.

Still a few pieces!

I pulled up the edge of my T-shirt and cleaned them off, blowing hard so the flakes didn't stick to the cloth.

My hands looked clean now, but I could still feel the sensation of the skull. I seriously doubted the sinks worked, but I looked around for a drinking fountain. There was one a few gates down, and I ran to it and jabbed at the bar. Nothing.

Fuck!

I stumbled backwards, feeling lightheaded and dazed.

Pulling the water bottle out of my bag, I doused my hands, rubbing them madly on my pants. Swiveling my head left and right, I chose a direction and ran.

THAT WAS UNEXPECTED

Time passed. I thought I'd been three days, but I wasn't sure. The water bottle in my bag was long since drained, the two protein bars were eaten, and I was starting to feel weak and dehydrated. I drifted in and out of sleep, spending my waking moments wandering the labyrinth of the airport. The Hudson News shops usually had food, but somehow, they are all devoid of this. Just paper. Inedible glossy paeans to the worldwide obsession with the latest celebrities

I couldn't seem to find my original gate, and all the others had locked doors. I couldn't locate any evidence of an entrance or exit. Which was strange. They were usually clearly marked. The tarmac outside gleamed with the passing of light, slightly bluer in the morning, more of a dying yellow in the evening, but I saw nothing else except concrete, and a farther rim of grass. The glass was unbreakable. I know. I'd tried.

My desperate frenzy of the first few days had degenerated into a resigned shuffle as I slowly trekked down hallway after hallway. It was probably midafternoon when as I rounded a corner and my heart practically jumped into my throat.

"Oh my god... Who are you?"

A desperate looking woman gasped, backing away in terror. Wearing a solemn black business suit, a mess of dark brown hair cradled her attractive, slightly olive-skinned face.

"I... I don't know."

Thoughts rushed through my head in a blur. I couldn't quite think of the right words, how to not make this lady scared of me, yet address the strangeness of the situation.

"What are you doing here?"

"Uh... where am I?"

With that, my heart sank. She was in the same situation as me. I debated what to tell her and settled on my middle name.

"Jon."

"I'm Alicia. What is this place?"

"What's the last thing you remember?"

"I was asleep, on a plane. When I woke up, I was here..."

"On a plane? You don't remember anything else?"

"No... I... Should I?"

"Where, specifically, were you?"

"Just... on a plane..."

She looked a little nervous. Then again, she was probably a bit disoriented. Her situation was probably way beyond her understanding. It was a mystery to me, but I'd bet it was more earth-shattering to her.

"I'm... just as lost as you. I have no idea what is going on. I've spent the past three days wandering these halls. I've seen no sign of life. I'm hungry, thirsty, and I miss my morning coffee."

With that, her face seemed to relax a little.

"I... I have a big bottle of Evian water in my purse... I always carry it with me when I fly... You're welcome to some..."

She dug it out of her bag and held it up. Most of a 20-ounce bottle, and I was parched! I graciously took a swig, careful not to guzzle down too much. It might have to last. It almost hurt, dissolving the hardened lump my throat had become.

"Thank you... I needed that. You want to join me? I haven't found anything, but at least the two of us can keep each other from blindly going down paths we've already tread."

She looked a little uncertain.

"Look, two heads are better than one, and I don't know about you, but I can use the company."

I didn't mention that it also didn't hurt that she was attractive. She looked down at her feet for a moment, not returning my gaze. A minute passed. Then another.

"Um... alright."

And with that, we started out, following the same trail I'd been wandering for days.

A WOMAN'S TOUCH

Day one, we slept in separate rows and walked a foot apart, barely saying a word to each other. Halfway through the day, she begrudgingly held out a Cliff bar. Pulling out another for herself, she proceeded to nibble on it gingerly. It struck me how much people were like rodents. Not really doing much that didn't feed some basic survival need. Clever little animals, just interested in building a better burrow, hording up a slightly larger cache of nuts than the other guy. Pathetic.

Day two, we were both just sitting down, wishing we had some food or water. At least that's what I was wishing. She had three Cliff bars. One she gave me, and the last one she broke in two so we could share it. I got the feeling she didn't really want to, but I was right there, and she probably felt guilty. That was early this morning. I was starving then, but I'd gone without food so long now that I was almost not hungry again. My energy at a low ebb, she broke down as we rested. In fact, she just burst out with this agitated rant about her life.

She's from Chicago. Her mom and dad are from Sicily, but they hate each other. She's the product of a broken home and has managed to pass that on to her own generation. By her account, her ex-husband is a spiky haired, football- and beer-loving douche-bag. Only too happy to leave her at home while he was out at the bar. Or wherever he really was. She had her doubts. Unfortunately, she had kids. Two, a boy and a girl, one five and one three. She had to move out of her formerly comfortable middle-class house and into a small place complete with a roommate (a girlfriend she has known most of her life). It was a tragedy for her, but nothing that didn't happen a million times a day. Despite that, she'd really grown on me. In attraction at least. She had a cute little way to her. Dark hair that fell in curved strands across her face. Little dimples that distorted otherwise perfect skin as she talked. She was obviously educated and well spoken. I thought I would really make a go for her, in another time and place. If she didn't have kids. Kids were a hassle, worse than roommates. I lived alone for a reason. I thought about asking her where she was going, traveling from Chicago, but I really didn't care.

THREE DAYS LATER

Her water was gone, her snacks long since devoured by both of us. The halls had a creepiness to them. They say one of the surest signs of a supernatural sighting is your senses put you on edge. You feel the presence of something else. There were areas of the corridors that had that element to them. The walls were a little darker, the shadows a little more tangible. I knew she felt it too, because she pulled me closer at those spots. I could smell her fear. Times like this, it didn't matter how attractive she was. I didn't want to die like this. With her. I felt unsung, like I'd backed into a corner with a simpleton as my only consolation. I felt... I don't know…. like I needed something more…

But it wears at you. Hour after hour. Skin prickling, back hairs rising. Then hours of mindless tedium. A sort of delirium set in. The lack of food and water making me lightheaded. My physical strength ebbed and flowed. My voice, on the rare times I used it, had grown husky with the lack of hydration. Drafts of cold, causing my skin to break out in goose bumps, flowed over my body on a regular basis. I didn't even know if it was real, or a result of the state of confusion I'd degenerated into. I didn't trust my hearing any longer. I'd jerked in panic at noises that she swore she never heard.

By the end of the day, we were two crushed people walking hand in hand. Night was falling, and we were growing tired. Truth be told, we'd been tired since the fitful bout of sleep we made it through last night. But with the failing of the sunlight, it seemed as good a time as any for the day to draw to a close. As we rounded a corner, three halls met, and we took the one to the right. Nothing new, we'd seen the split before, and it never seemed to lead anywhere. As we walked down the new corridor, looking for a gate that looked a little more inviting than most so we could camp for the night, she suddenly shrieked.

I almost jumped, fully awake now. Following her outstretched finger, my gaze traveled until it landed on... nirvana! Well, I'd take what I could get, and this looked like nirvana to me. A daybed! The kind they roll out for overnight travelers that missed their connection, complete with thin sheet and crappy airline pillow.

My body was sore and out of sorts, and I felt numb, but I debated who would get the bed? I was thinking I should be the gentleman. She started toward it, kicking off her shoes, sitting down, and wrapping herself with the sheet. Closing her eyes for a moment she re-opened them and looked up blissfully. I felt a twinge of anger.

She's going to take it. Just like that?

Her gaze fell on me. She raised her hand and beckoned. I paused, but only for a moment. Stepping forward, I pulled off my Vans, hoping my feet don't stink too much, and climbed onto the cot. She maneuvered around, pulling off her dress coat. Then she unbuttoned and took off her shirt. Smooth, silky skin flowed under a lacy white bra. The shirt had hidden a lot. Nice, full B cups. I started to pull off my T-shirt, and she unclasped her bra. Half-dollar-size aureoles, crowned by erect nipples greeted me. The textured bumps encircling them reminding me of the cold in the air. I felt a stir. Not just in my loins, but my whole body. I know we were in a nightmare of a situation, but all I could think of was how much I wanted this. My former lethargy seemed to have retreated, desire taking over. She tugged at my jeans, and I reached for the waistband to pull them off. When I looked up again...

She was so beautiful! Well-toned and almost completely shaved. A few days' growth, but what could you expect. I leaned over to embrace her, kissing her passionately and then moving on to gently bite at her neck. Her hair smelled of cinnamon and spice, even after days without a shower. I didn't feel tired, I didn't feel hungry. I just had the most beautiful sex I'd ever had in my life.

When we were done, the hunger and thirst started to come back, but I felt more content than I had in a very long time. We snuggled into bed together, spooning each other under the thin white sheet. I smiled with her soft breath on my shoulder and nodded off.

OPEN YOUR EYES

A sharp pain startled me. Piercing, as if a raw nerve had been struck at the base of my scalp. I tried to raise my hands, but they were dead weight. I tried to scream, but my mouth was already wide open, thin streams of saliva seeping out. My eyes still worked, and I rotated them right and left in their sockets. I was still lying sideways on the cot, the sheet covering most of my body, but I couldn't feel anything!

Only this horrible pain! Like a jackhammer to the back of my head!

Then I heard a liquid slurp, and my world grew fuzzy. The shining plastic and knitted padding of the seats in front of me resolved back into focus, my image growing sharper as the fluorescent glare burned into my eyes. I heard a soft padding and cluster of hisses coming from behind. Then I caught a slight glimpse...

Was that her?

Orange globes, the irises slit down the middle like a reptile, stared back at me. A trickle of blood trailed down from her mouth, half-dried in mid drip as it fell off her chin. Her lips twisted up into a smile, opening just enough to reveal long, thin rows of needle-like teeth. A forked tongue lashed out, slurping away some of the blood on her chin.

What the fuck I should have been able to see... to notice... something...

Pain shot through the back of my head. I heard another slurp, and everything went black.

BACK ON BOARD THE PLANE

A plane had docked at JFK, and a woman was screaming. She woke up to the shriveled remains of a corpse reclining beside her. Airport security came running. She couldn't remember exactly what he looked like. After all, who pays attention to most fellow travelers?

" Middle aged man, seemed a little quiet and cold."

It almost makes the papers. Almost. Time passes. People forget. They seem only too eager. In a world of seven billion, people go missing all the time. And there are things that like it better that way.

DR. SEUSS IS DEAD

EARLY MORNING

Blinding sunlight washes over as I throw off the covers. Rubbing the sleep from my eyes, I climb down from the top bunk. My brother used to have the lower one, but he has his own room now.

Summer 1987. I have a whole three months until I have to go back to school again! I think I'll head downtown. Hit Walmart and K-mart, see if there is anything worth stealing. Maybe hit the comic shop, too, then head over to Kevin's.

Fumbling through the dresser, I pull out my favorite T-shirt. Fading and worn at the seams, the glow-in-the-dark skeleton crowned by the moniker "Metallica" has seen more than a little criticism at the hands of my hyper-religious mom. Slipping on my shorts, I bend down and run my hand under the dresser, groping for my cigarettes. They are not too hard to score at the university vending machine, but I look even younger than my 14 years, and I dread getting caught every time. Stuffing them in my waistband, I flip my shirt over, slip on my backpack, socks and tennis shoes, and head downstairs.

"Hi, honey. I see you're up."

Ugh. She makes me cringe every time. Mid-thirties, and she's decided it's time to get braces. She looks like an updated Little House on the Prairie mom, all sweetness and homilies. But I know the evil that lies within. I've lived with it all my life.

Heading out the side door and into the garage, I scoop up my blue Schwinn, fish headphones out of my pack, and hit play on the cassette deck. Rolling up the shaded driveway, the opening strains of *Ride The Lightening* kick in. I spill out onto the main road and as I start to gain speed, bright sunlight pours in through the canopy of branches. Coating me in mottled shafts of white as I pass. The trees retreat farther back as the road heads towards the highway, and the early summer heat of northern Florida kicks in. The fresh scent of pine fills the air, just as a crescendo of heavy riffing supplants the acoustic intro of *"Fight Fire with Fire."* As I skid out on the main thoroughfare, I glance over at a work man across the street that's re-pouring a block of the concrete walkway.

"Hey, kid, you know who did this?"

He looks pissed, probably cleaning up the fresh block we tagged last night. I shake my head and pedal on, heading towards the 7-11. He looks after me with obvious disbelief.

After a few feet, the 7-11 pops up. I pull my bike up to the sidewall and flip the kickstand. Heading in, the Indian guy at the counter gives me the evil eye. I don't even think he knows how ridiculous he looks, all dolled up with neatly coiffed black hair and a comically red work shirt.

I sidle up to the soda fountain and fill up a Super Big Gulp with Big Red. Slipping into the next aisle, I scan for batteries. I need them for my Walkman, not to mention the Lazer Tag set I stole last week. Spotting a pack of AAs, I pop them out of the blister pack, and with a little sleight of hand, they now reside in my waistband. Strolling nonchalantly up to the counter, I set down the soda and twirl around my backpack to look for money. With a thud, the batteries fall out and bounce across the floor. I freeze, my face burning red as I tilt up to make eye contact with the clerk. He lets out a half-hiss, half-sigh, and says-

"I'll take those."

I pick them up and drop the batteries on the counter. Throwing out a dollar, I grab the Big Gulp and make a quick exit. I don't wait for change, and don't look back, yet I can almost feel his stare as I exit. Rounding the corner, I jump on my bike and take off.

A block down, the walkway dives into a field of wild grass, an abandoned plot that splits up into a maze of concrete pathways through groves of tall weeds. The winding outskirts of a shopping center abandoned years ago. The whole lot is huge and has a desolate feel to it. It's one of my favorite places. I trundle down a winding path until I'm well out of sight of the road and pull over. Dropping my bike, I nestle amid a thrush of tall blades and draw out a cigarette. Lighting a match and taking a deep pull, I slowly sit down. A head rush kicks in on schedule as I squat on the sand. Wind whistles through the grass, the leaves rustling and tossing free chaff.

The air has a magical quality to it. Rolling tracts of gossamer clouds trail through the field of blue overhead, writhing and tumbling in giant banks of moisture. I feel truly alone out here, like I'm isolated in an abandoned land far away from the constraints of my military dad and hellhole of a home.

Dad was in usual form last night, chasing me through the house, pinning me down and taking stabs at my long hair with a pair of scissors. It's barely touching my shoulders, but still much too long for his conservative neurosis. I pierced my ear with a safety pin a few days ago and weaved a single thread through it so the hole won't close. He noticed, and yelled at me, trying to snatch the string from my ear.

I have to do something. I just don't know what. I've tried to run away twice, and they just track me down at the shelter, tell them I'm lying, and haul me home. He has to protect his precious image in the community. I have three more years. It seems like a lifetime.

They had fliers in my school, local fast-food restaurants reaching out for summer employees. Plenty of people took them up on it, but I'm not ready to live in that box. I may be broke, but at least I'm free. Crushing the butt into the ground, I stand up and brush off my ass. Sand everywhere. I don't know how anything grows here. The roots beneath me even swarm over top of one another in a morass of desperation. This all used to be underwater, I hear, centuries ago. Maybe it still should be. Clean out some of the riff raff. Which would be almost everyone in this state.

Emerging from the brush, I hop on my bike and head out.

THE HAZZARDS OF COMMERCE

I roll up to Walmart, park my bike, and stroll in. Sauntering down the music aisle, I scan the shelves for anything good. Ratt. Quiet Riot. Lots of stuff I was into last year, but none of my new favorites. I already snagged a couple of Metallica albums, and one Megadeth, from the K-mart across town. Out of boredom, more than anything else, I pry open a security box, and snatch up Alice Cooper and Def Leppard albums. I wouldn't want the trip to be a total waste. Nonchalantly traipsing out of the front doors, I've dropped my bag and am about to mount my bike when I hear:

"I did it! I did it! You caught me!"

A fat black woman is being tackled by a police officer. He shoots me a look and mutters-

"I hope you didn't steal anything."

I shake my head, hop on the bike, and take off. The same burning feeling I had in the 7-11 is prickling the back of my neck and I'm spooked. I decide to skip the K-mart and head straight to Kevin's.

BACKWOODS LIFE

An hour across town, and I wheel onto the dirt road that leads up to Kevin's house. Grooves of packed mud trundle through the dense field of underbrush that leads up to his mobile home. Nestled on the outskirts of woods owned by his uncle, it was some family deal struck up to help a young single mom.

Kevin's mom's blue Honda Accord isn't parked out front, which means we won't have to sneak onto the roof to smoke or drink beer! I drop the bike, ascend the wooden steps, and am about to knock when Kevin swings open the door. He's skinny and tall, with the thin beginnings of a mustache adorning his upper lip. It looks ridiculous, but whatever.

"Hey, Jay! What's up?"

"Hey, Kevin, your mom at work?"

"Yeah, she's at the hospital until 8:00."

"Sweet."

With that, I'm ushered in, and we proceed to pop on Robocop. Grabbing a Coors Light from the fridge, he pulls out a deck of cards, and we sit down in front of the TV to begin our usual game. Betting for comic books. I always cheat. I'm sure Kevin does as well, but I'm better at it than he is!

A few hours pass, and we've made it through Robocop, Texas Chainsaw Massacre 2, and most of Friday the 13th part 3. We can't drink any more beers without it being obvious. We're both tired of playing cards, and Kevin's a little mad that I won his first appearance of Wolverine. So, we head out to explore the woods.

"Let's head over to that construction site."

"What construction site?"

"The one I saw on the road in. It's off to the left. Bunch of old concrete tunnels and shit."

"Never been there."

"Really?"

He shrugs his shoulders. Kevin's a bit weird like that. The place has probably been there for years, and he never even bothered to check it out. I scoop up the skateboard behind his couch and we head out.

THE OLD CONSTRUCTION SITE

I t's a cool landscape of crumbling stone. Rusting iron bars jut out from cracked blocks of concrete. Sections of giant stone sewer tubes lie forsaken amidst the rubble. We lounge in one and smoke, the light of the sun slowly growing yellow as it passes over the broken landscape.

"I noticed an underground sewer line at the edge of the site."

"So."

"So, let's check it out!"

"And how do you propose we do that?"

"I'll take the skateboard, lay flat on my stomach, and roll in!"

"Sounds retarded."

"Whatever. You sit here. I'm going to explore!"

Grabbing the board, I wander out into the sunlight and begin traipsing through the debris. A few minutes later Kevin follows.

A conduit of dusty stone is buried in the side of an embankment. I set the skateboard down inside the tunnel, crawl in, and lay on top. Pressing my hands against the concrete walls, I propel myself forward. After a few feet, a dim blue light emerges from the farther reaches, and I head for it. Blackness closes in, the air dry and desiccating as if it were a living thing. Maybe I've been watching too many horror movies. A sense of claustrophobia creeps in, and I turn my head to peer back. Nothing but darkness. I try to turn more, but there's no space. I fight back a wave of panic.

There's nothing to worry about! I can go back the way I came, just push myself backwards!

After what seems forever the glow grows stronger and appears to be coming from around the next bend. I struggle forward, the wheels catching and slowing on the sand that litters the tunnel. My arms are growing tired, but I keep pushing. I want to know where that light is coming from. I can rest better if this opens up into a larger space.

As I close in, the air grows cool and thin. I start to feel uncomfortable and trapped. Pinching my eyes tight, I shove forward with all my might. On the third try, I hear a crunch of sand, and my eyes pop open as the wheels beneath me drop an inch.

I'm in an underground chamber!

The dark gaps of the tunnel glare at me from opposite sides but the room I've stumbled into is high and round. The floor is coated in dead leaves and dirt, a thin, gleaming ring of light filtering down. A series of rusted metal rungs scale up towards what must be a manhole. I crawl to my feet, grab the deck, and walk over. As I pass through the center of the pit, the hairs on the back of my neck stand up. I whirl around, staring at the tunnel I came through.

Something feels off. I need to get out of here. I don't dare re-enter that tunnel, I'll have to try going up!

Collaring a rung, I tuck the deck under my arm, and start climbing.

It turns out to be much farther than it looked. I peer back down, but the glare of the overhead light must be blinding me. I keep climbing. My shoulders ache and my hand grows tired. I switch the deck to my other arm, make it a few more rungs and start to wear down again.

This is no good. I'll have to lose the board.

I let go, the deck clanging against the walls as it disappears into the depths. I listen for it to land, but there's no crash. It must have hit those leaves or something. I resume climbing. The going is faster now that I have two hands, and it isn't long before I run up against the ceiling.

I can't make out any features, just the pale circular gleam. Funny, it seemed much brighter far below. I press against it but it doesn't move. I push harder. Still nothing. It's probably rusted in place. I doubt anyone has accessed this in decades. Scrambling closer, I press the back of my head against the manhole cover. Cold metal bites back, and I grit my teeth. I press harder still and notice a slight rustle. Gasping in a few breaths first, I try again. A slow creak is followed by it breaking open and showering me with flakes of rust. Some gets in my eye. Blinking rapidly, my vision blurry through a veil of watery grit, I make out the yellowish light of late afternoon.

I could have sworn that light had a cooler tone down in the tunnel. Maybe it's something to do with the depth.

I shove aside the manhole cover and crawl onto the lip. Resting for a moment, I scan my surroundings.

It looks like a continuation of the construction site. I'm on a jagged little island of concrete anchored by a manhole. I must be atop some small hill, as chunks of stone descend into the troughs below. Embankments of dirt rise on the sides, the one in front trailing across the ditch and into a chain link fence. I think I saw that fence from the other side, which means that a road lies beyond.

As I crawl up to the edge of embankment, I see that it's steeper up close. Too steep to descend. But there are some roots jutting out of a nearby broken pillar.

Fuck it.

I crouch down and jump at a protruding root. Grasping with both hands, I try to twist into a desperate swing. Apparently with not enough momentum, as I swing back. My arm is starting to ache and I switch grips in midair. Pushing off the pillar again, this time it's enough and my fingers wrap around links of metal. They quickly start to burn as the thin wire cuts into me, but I'm stubborn. Letting go of the root and clutching with my other hand, I pull myself up farther.

As I scale the links, the fence groans and starts to bend backwards. I keep hoisting myself up, desperately peering at the top and hoping the fence holds.

Finally, my searching hand rises for the next link and instead I feel the top. With renewed vigor, I pull myself over, lose my grip, and tumble over.

It's only a few feet and I land on a cushion of weeds. Panting hard, I slowly catch my breath as I look around. I was right. This is just on the other side of that road. I notice it's grown dark, and I wonder how much time has passed.

Is Kevin still in the yard? Does he think I'm lost?

I stagger out onto the dirt road. It's become much cooler out, and I fold my arms as I head towards the trailer.

THE INABILITY OF THE HUMAN MIND

The trees surrounding the camper seem unusually dark. They almost look alive, but maybe I'm just being paranoid. It's all those horror movies. A breeze cuts through, ruffling the sleeves of my T-shirt and tearing at the folds of my shorts. I rub my arms and lean forward as I enter the trees. The lights are on in Kevin's house but it's not fully dark yet, so his mom can't be home. I start to feal real uneasy.

I really hope I don't have to go back to the site for Kevin.

Scaling the steps, I notice the screen door is closed, but the main door is slightly cracked and emitting a thin strip of light.

"Hello?"

I bang on the metal frame. Nothing.

"Hello?"

I wait for a minute, but still nothing. I inch open the screen door and give the main door a gentle push.

"Hello?"

A TV is on, the glare illuminating the back of a couch. It's been moved in front of the TV, and a person sits there.

"Kevin?"

No response. Nightmare scenarios start running through my head.

He's dead! It's not him, it's some stranger!

Then I hear some movie theme I sort of recognize. His head shifts, his hand holding aloft a small plastic box.

"Hello?"

This guy sounds a bit like Kevin, but the voice is a bit deeper and raspier.

"Hey, Jen. Yeah, nothing. Just watching TV, having a beer. What? Yeah."

Who is he talking to? He's just holding up that box. I don't hear anyone else.

I move closer.

"Mister?"

He's ignoring me!

He starts to get up, and I dive into a nearby closet, pulling the blind shut as I nestle in amidst shoes and hanging garments. His footfalls grow closer. The the door swings open and my eyelids peel wide as I struggle to back deeper into the closet. But there is nowhere to go.

The man is a dead ringer for Kevin! Twenty years older, and missing a lot of hair, but the face is the same! Is that his dad?

And then he does something impossible. He reaches right through me, picks up a pair of boots, and turns away. Still holding that little piece of plastic up to his ear. He walks over to the couch, bends down for a moment, comes up with a narrower but longer small black box and pushes something on it. The TV dies. Just like that.

"Alright, Jen. See you in a bit."

With that, he stuffs the plastic box he was talking to in his jeans, pulls out a set of keys, and heads towards the door. Still sitting in the closet, anchored in fear and disbelief, I watch him walk out.

THINGS GET WORSE

A couple minutes pass. I hear him descend the steps, crunch across the gravel, and open a car door. The door slams shut, the engine turns over a few times, the vehicle roars to life and spins out in a rasp of flying stone.

There was no car there earlier. I didn't see one when I came in, but it was dark out.

The rumble of the muffler slowly fades away, until all is silent again except for the rush of wind and scrape of pine needles. The gusts sound more strained than usual, and I'm terrified to move, but too anxious to stay still.

Finally I scramble to my feet and cautiously peer around the closet doorframe. In front of me is a black TV, way larger and thinner than any I've ever seen before, and a coffee table blanketed by a mess of magazines.

Maxim magazine? I've never heard of that before. Must be new.

Off to the right, faintly illuminated by a light from the kitchen, is an odd-looking table. Mounted by a keypad, it resembles the kind I have in the computer room at school.

Only it has a slender, dark screen immediately behind that's way too thin to be a computer. A hallway behind the strange table leads off to Kevin's room. I head that way, curtailing my breath as every step is becomes a measured act of tension.

As I pass the couch, a chill envelops me. I shudder and take another step forward. It disappears. I step back, and the cold hits me again. I step forward. It fades away. It's then that I hear a slight rustle from the direction of Kevin's room.

Fuck this!

Swiveling around, I run towards the outside door.

It's wide open, the screen swinging softly in the wind.

That was closed! I watched it shut and lock!

I tear out, flying down the steps in almost a single jump. I don't dare forge deeper into the woods.

The dirt road! It's dark, but I can just make out the tire grooves!

I head for it, almost tripping as I plow through small gullies I can't see. My heart is racing in my chest. My breath comes in short bursts. I'm sure something must be back there! A dim swath of light hits me and I jerk to the left.

I'm in the middle of a road now, the glare of headlights drowning me in a blaze of brilliance. I scream out, twist to run, but it's too late. As the truck hits, I screw my eyes closed.

I feel a slight breeze, but that's it. No painful crunch. No buckling metal.

I open my eyes to an empty black road. As I spin around, I see taillights receding down the highway.

What just happened?

I start to jog after the truck, slowly at first, then picking up pace as it recedes. Everything being dark except those taillights, I feel that if they disappear, I'll be lost.

The truck swerves a bit then suddenly angles sharply to the right and plows into a tree. I break from a run into a full-on sprint.

It takes a good five minutes, but as I draw up, I can see that the front end is crumpled around a pine tree. The headlights are both still on, throwing beams around the assailing trunk and into the woods beyond. Twin red orbs glow from the tail, their position in virtual darkness giving them the illusion of floating. I open the passenger door and can see that the windshield is buckled outwards in a labyrinth of spiderwebs. A sheen of blood, much darker than the Hollywood variety, is splattered across the glass. It saturates the shift lever and emergency brake as it tracks out through an open door.

The driver must have wandered out into the woods. I need to call the cops or something. But I don't even know exactly where I am! The closest house I know is Kevin's, and I'm terrified of going back there!

A scream pierces the silence, followed by a wet crunch.

Oh, fuck! Oh, fuck...

I start running. Away from the glowing wreckage, away from whatever horror lies there. Away into the dark.

IT'S ONLY THE END OF THE WORLD

All I hear are the soles of my feet striking the pavement. Something shifts overhead, and a few stars become visible, their light scantily illuminating the roadway. There's a speck of light in the distance.

That must be a house! There must be someone home!

The smells of moist soil and dried grass swarm in, the wind picking up and reminding me of the cold sweat coating my armpits. My legs start to fatigue as I start to encounter more resistance and stumble more. The trail must have become a dirt road. As the light slowly nears, my gasps become hoarse and shallow. I slow and hold my breath for a second, but I hear no indication of pursuit.

Maybe I lost whatever it was in the dark!

Then my skin turns cold, and I slow. It's Kevin's trailer. I don't know what to do.

As I approach the front steps, I hear a rustle in the underbrush, and jump back.

What the fuck was that!

But there's nothing. The cold starts to bite into my cooling skin. I keep standing still. For what seems forever.

I can't stay here all night! Maybe if I make a dash for the front door? Wait a minute, the door is closed! I left it wide open! That means someone must be home!

I sprint at the door, swivel the knob, and plunge inside.

That old man is back! Nestled on the couch with some fuggly looking girl!

Then I realize-

They haven't even noticed me!

"Hey."

No response. The TV must be drowning me out. The broadcaster looks strange. His hair is military short, the suit super bland but trim and tight.

"Here at the 2011 World Championships, it looks like..."

2011? Is that the name of the championship? I don't know anything about sports.

"Hey!"

I call out again, louder this time.

They still don't hear me!

I step forward and approach the couch.

Something in the far corner moves, and I glance over. It looks still now. I must be seeing things. The shifting light of the TV must be distorting my vision. Then I hear a sort of low, clicking sound.

What the fuck?

I stare back at the shadows.

Are they shifting? Just a little bit?

I rub my eyes. Nothing.

Suddenly, a long, ebony tendril shoots outs, coiling in on itself as a few more creep out to greet it.

Fuck!

"Hey, mister!"

I yell, but he doesn't seem to hear me.

"Mister!"

I scream louder, but neither of them react!

The tentacle creeping out of the corner hasn't moved forward. It just twitches and sways, a multitude of other little nubs joining in. I don't want to get any closer, but I have to warn them!

I dash in front. Blocking out the TV. I jump up and down, waving my arms.

In the light of the TV, the man resembles even more an older version of Kevin. It must be his father.

Wait a minute... Why am I not casting a shadow over them?

"Hey!"

With a moist scraping a noise emanates from the corner. I peer over and the tentacles seem agitated.

They are moving more and seem to be inching closer. A fetid odor wafts over, and I lose it. Screaming, I run out the door, making a mad dash towards the highway.

As I stumble through a trough, a full moon breaks out, blanketing the field in an eerie glow. I suddenly recall the crashed truck.

Are they everywhere? It wasn't like this until I came out of that tunnel! Maybe I should head there. I'm done for if I stay out here!

I try to scan ahead, looking for the chain-link fence. Nothing yet, but I think it's up ahead. Funny how you don't really pay attention to landmarks until you're lost.

I dare a quick look back. Everything is dark except for the shrinking glow of the doorway. I stumble again, twisting my knee with the quick rebound, and vow to not look again. Just pour on the steam. Up on the left, emerging out of the brush, is the fence!

One section looks freshly trampled.

That must be from me!

I make it over the fence in a desperate scramble and only remember the drop after I'm hanging on the other side by my fingertips.

If I can just make it through that channel below and scale back up to the manhole, I'll have a chance.

I don't think the drop is too steep. Bringing my knees to my stomach, I let go.

As I smack into dirt, I tumble over and a rock tears into my knee.

"Fuck!"

Paralyzed by pain, I rock back and forth.

I can't stay here! That thing—or things, whatever they are—surely heard me! I have to move.

I rise and nearly fall over as pain shoots up my leg. My foot is on fire, but I manage to limp forward. Throwing my hands up onto the slab of concrete, I pull myself up. My ankle is throbbing and puffing up already.

But if I stop I'm dead!

The gaping maw of the manhole is still open. I peer down but can't make out anything. I run my hands down the sides, feeling for the rungs.

Bingo!

As my hand closes around one, a scraping noise cuts through the hum of crickets and I bolt upright as I scan the trench behind me. Boulders and iron spikes protrude out of the shadows. Something moving glistens in the depths. The moon breaks out of the cloud cover and illuminates the recesses.

There must be millions of them!

They look like huge worms... only sickly green, the mouth a grotesque tangle of needle-sharp teeth. I swivel around in panic.

They're everywhere, all around me!

A cadaverous stench wafts up. I flip into panic mode and scramble into the manhole. My feet keep slipping, but I don't dare slow down. Every strike of my right foot brings a stab of pain but I try to ignore it.

My feet slam into the concrete floor, and I drop to my knees. I feel around for the skateboard.

Where is it! Fuck!

The noises get louder... a revolting wet slithering. I desperately scramble around, my hands clawing through partially dried mud.

Nothing! I have to move. If those things reach the edge and start dropping, I'm fucked! Left... I think I need to go left...

I crawl up to the wall and feel along until it falls in. Ducking my head down I wriggle into the narrow tube.

I can't rise above my knees, but with an awkward mix of clawing at the walls and shuffling forward, I manage to move. Scraping skin off my knuckles, I almost don't feel it. My heart beats a million miles an hour and sweat beads on my forehead. The air is grubby and oppressive. I don't remember any of this from when I came in.

My knee feels raw... I think I've ground off all the skin. I'm cramping up trying to keep it from rubbing against the floor, and grimacing in pain every time it does. My fingertips have developed blisters and are starting to smart as well. I feel like I can't keep going... but every time I start to slow, the stark terror of those worm things grips me, and I double my effort. Sweat trickles down my forehead and into my mouth. Followed by a grungy, fowl tang. I raise my head and cry out in pain as it slams into the ceiling.

Fuck! Fuck! I hate my life!

Tears well up, but I keep shuffling forward.

This has to end. I have to reach something!

IT'S ALL DOWNHILL FROM HERE

Nightmares. I'm running through the aisles of a grocery store. Shelves of food tower over me, their glossy plastic sheaths glimmering under the florescent glare. As I duck behind a stack of cardboard boxes, two soldiers, swathed in tan military uniforms, bark orders at each other. Their shoulders are decorated in cords of red, their grimy faces half-hidden under the brims of cadet hats.

Eventually their combat boots shuffle down the glistening river of polished tile, and away from my hiding spot.

They are looking for me. The rapture has come, they are soldiers of the anti-Christ, and I've been left behind. I don't know how I know that, but it's unquestionable... and terrifying. Every nerve is on fire.

"Over there!"

I hear one call out, and without looking, I take off. I'm running as fast as I can, but my legs are moving so slowly...

"Jason."

My eyes pop open. I'm in a bed, in a hospital. I start to move my hand but feel a painful tug. A tube is sticking out of my left forearm. My mom is at the foot of the bed, eying me with quizzical reproach. She doesn't say anything, just shakes her head in disdain.

"Mom... where am I?"

"The hospital. They found you severely dehydrated and unconscious, your body covered in scrapes and bruises. I told you that Kevin boy was no good. Were you smoking weed with him?"

"No! I... I was just exploring the construction site..."

"Oh, I know, that's where they found you. Robin called the paramedics."

"Yeah? But I didn't smoke anything! Kevin didn't do anything! I went down a drainage tunnel, and there were... monsters on the other side!"

"Hmph. You know better than to call me mom. What are you on? Were you watching horror movies again? Listening to that Satanic music?"

"No, mom!"

"It's the devil. He works in mischievous ways. Filling your head with—"

"No, mom! You don't understand!"

"I understand that you are banned from Kevin's house."

"No, but he didn't—"

And with that, she turns and walks out. I know what I saw. And there might be evil in this world, but the Devil had nothing to do with it. I haven't believed in a god for years. But this... this goes deeper. I feel tired. Drained. My head rolls back, and I start to doze off.

NOTHING GETS BETTER WITH AGE

It's been years, and I left Florida long ago. I haven't seen or even really thought about Kevin since that day, two decades past. Life has a way of sweeping your past under a carpet of time, making you forget. It doesn't get better; the details just blur with age.

People walk around with cell phones now. They spend way too much of their time on home computers. It never really struck me, until just recently, that the common, everyday items I see bandied about by the citizens of today are the same as those I saw so long ago. In my dream, or whatever it was.

Two nights ago, I started out of bed. Drenched in sweat, the dreary pre-dawn light painting the room, my heaving chest gleaming with moisture, I had a revelation.

I threw aside the covers, rubbed my eyes, and knew what I had to do. This world isn't real. These people, this apartment, my car... none of it. Not real in the sense that people think it is. We're just a speck. A ripple in the timeline of history. And you know what? Some of us aren't even the genuine article. There are monsters out there. Pretending to be people. Or maybe the people really are the monsters. Not that it matters.

A box of ammo thumps down on the gleaming countertop. As fluorescent light bathes me, the clerk thumps his fingers.

"Here we are, sir. So you like that one?"

"Yeah, I think I'll take it."

"It's a nice rifle. Very accurate. Especially with that scope."

"That's what I want."

"You got some good game lined up?"

"I would say so."

"Good hunting then. You ready to be rung up?"

"Sure."

I stroll out of the gun store with pride. Shoulders straight, a big smile on my face, the wind rustles my hair. Multi-colored leaves flutter past, twisting and swirling as they skitter down the cobblestone. New England is so beautiful in the fall. The faint scent of burning hickory in the air, the heaped congregations of stone that separate the walkway from the trunks above. Their branches are aflame with the colors of autumn.

An iron fence, its rods curling up in Victorian elegance, emancipates the short stone walls from the forest beyond. An older woman, all white and pearls, passes. Smiling and waving. Such a nice day. Too bad it has to end in blood.

FORT BRAGG

Made in America

I would watch out of the second-floor window, eyes wide with attention, at the night glow that emanated from the ball court. I lived in a brick duplex, as did we all. The houses were stacked in a loose circle around one another, each occupied by a military family, and each looked exactly the same. None of that seemed weird. All of us kids just grew up together in military households. But late at night, in the gloom and shadows, I felt I was in some strange isolation. Shining through my window like a beacon, the bright light of the ball court seemed to call to me.

It was really nothing, just a fenced-in basketball court wedged in between a small asphalt path and woods that were mostly pine, the grounds beneath lumpy and overgrown in a blanket of brush and dead needles. As kids we would play soldier in those woods, shooting bottle rockets out of empty hairspray canisters at each other. We all noticed that the further you delved into the trees, the more remnants of old training grounds popped up. Foundations of long since demolished buildings. Half-filled in foxholes and trenches. It was basically an unspoken agreement that something creepy lingered there. We'd laugh and scamper around the edges, but no one dared step quite into the ruins. Maybe it was superstition. Maybe we'd all seen one too many horror movies. But in the dark, alone in my bed, the harsh light of that ball court gleaming in through my window, something felt off. Sinister. Creepy.

I traveled the path that led by it all the time. The trail wandered out onto the main road, and I'd often walk it to the local 7-11 to grab some candy or a comic book. In the day it was just part of another dilapidated ball court. But at night. At night it seemed sinister. It gave me a gut feeling that lingered on through the night.

I had to be in by 18:00 or my parents would yell at me. I'd often creep to the door after bedtime and read comics by the sliver of light. The Shadow was a favorite of mine, I even had a poster of him on my wall. It was the only poster they let me pin to the wall, and even that was a struggle. Regardless, in the dark, crouched by the door, that beam from the ball court was always present. It pierced through the window and most nights it would draw me to the glass.

One day, feeling unusually adventurous, I determined that I was going to sneak out and prove to myself there was nothing to that whole light thing after all. It had been bothering me for months, and I decided that was insane.

I tried to climb out through my window but it was too much. I was a small kid at 12, and that drop from the roof above the porch looked too steep. So I waited. Waited until I was sure my parents were asleep.

Burning with tension, I watched their room from across the hall for any movement. I decided it was now or never and I darted out, flew down the steps, cracked open the front door, and slipped into the darkness.

I waded through wet grass as I rounded the side of the house, and skipped up onto the trail that ran behind my small backyard fence. It's black asphalt surface glimmered even now in the light of the distant ball court. A soft wind kicked in, the smell of pine overwhelming, but something musty trickled behind it, crinkling my nose as I headed towards the distant light.

The trail passed through a small cove of trees, their black trunks swarming in around me as I passed, but that glow remained omnipresent, its beams penetrating the throng of trees like a knife through butter. As the path exited the small, wooded enclave, that light seemed to multiply in intensity. As did my sense of dread. I argued that this was all irrational, yet the beam kept beating down on me with ever growing ferocity as I drew in. A buzzing started to sound in my ears, my head was throbbing, and I felt strange and distant. Shielding my eyes with my fingers, I stumbled forward.

Floundering through increasingly higher wet grass, the luminescence faded slightly, and I hesitantly withdrew my hand. The sharp tang of damp vegetation assailed my senses, and I stumbled backwards as the dark hulks of trees swallowed me up.

Turning around frantically, it dawned on me that somehow, I had ended up in the woods behind the ball court. This was not where I wanted to be at all! Feeling isolated and vulnerable, I twisted in as I staggered back towards the light. The rusty chain link wall of the court sprang up in front of me, the tall blades of grass along its perimeter assaulting my bare legs. Worse still, I could feel a presence behind me! Something dark and creepy. Although maybe it was just my imagination.My skin itched with tension and I wanted be anywhere but here. My back was a cold array of goosebumps, all my muscles stiff and clammy in shock, the hair on the back of my neck erect with some preternatural fear.

A muffled sound escaped the woods behind me, and I ran. Ran for my life. Ran to the house, scaled the chain link fence, and clawed fiercely at the wooden pillar that rose into the patio rooftop below my window. Splinters dug into my fingers, and tears rolled down my eyes. I just managed to make it up, ply open my window, and crawl inside.

Morning

My fingers hurt as I dug splinters out the next morning. It all seemed ridiculous in the light of day.

After school, I traveled down that bike path, stopping at the ball court and staring at the woods. They were just woods. They looked a bit dark and even a little creepy, but

I'd been in them a million times. I needed to break this before it became a thing.

Crossing into the tall grass, I rounded the ball court and entered the woods.

They looked a little forlorn for sure, the ground blanketed in pine needles, bare trunks scaling up into the heavens, but this was all familiar. I stepped in, ascending the rising terrain as I crested a small hill. The other side dropped steeply, and I half-slid, half-stumbled down the embankment. The slope was mired with potholes, a layer of pine needles covering their presence, and I slowed my descent by grasping at small bushes as I slid. The drop bottomed out in a dirt path, one I could swear I'd traveled before, and I followed it towards what I assumed was the direction of my house. As I navigated the sandy ridges of the path, a dried-out puddle burst into a frenzy of activity, and I jumped back in alarm. Feeling silly when a closer examination revealed that it was just a concealed sinkhole full of baby frogs, their small forms all coming to life as I drew close.

After about 10 minutes I figured I was pretty close to my house and turned from the trail to scale the embankment. It turned out not to be easy, and I kept slipping on the pine needles as I grabbed at close -by shrubbery for support. The loamy odor of moist soil spurted out every time I tore out vegetation, a spray of black soil following suit.

When I finally reached the top, I was breathing heavily. Spread out in front of me was the distressed foundation of a long-since leveled building. No surprise, these littered the woods. They and foxholes were the remnants of World War Two training grounds. Or at least that was the rumor.

I huffed deeply, caught my breath, and drew in closer to the concrete foundation. It was just a wall of moss and mildew-encrusted stone, a shallow flight of stairs leading up to a rectangular slab of stained flooring. At least that's what I assumed. As I drew in closer I noticed that just under the stairs was a small opening. It was mid-afternoon, maybe around four, and no one expected me home. I figured, why not explore it? With my luck, it was nothing, but I'd always wonder.

As I dove into the task of clearing away the debris, I noticed a drift of pine needles crusted heavily around the side of the stairs. It took me a good half hour of shoveling but I uncovered a larger gully than I had originally surmised. Even more interesting, what looked like a rough wooden door was behind what must have been decades of half-decayed dross. The door was small, more like the gate to a small storage cabinet than anything, but I was curious. If this was a World War Two building, who knew what was down here? I remember reading a book where a kid found a letter in some old collection of library books, only to discover that it was from one of the founding fathers and worth a shitload. In all likelihood, there was nothing there, but imagine the possibilities! Secret war documents! Gas masks and really old weapons! The pawn shops by the base downtown would probably pay a fortune. They mostly had military stuff. My dad said that GIs always pawned their gear for some quick money, then had to buy it back later.

I spent what must have been another 15 minutes, the leaves turning into moist decaying sludge the further down I dug, but finally the door looked free enough to open. I tried and, of course, it wasn't. I climbed up over the now foul-smelling pile of wet soil and decayed pine needles I'd erected, found a fallen branch, and climbed back down again.

I dug at the black soil, the grime tearing away in black, rocky clumps, and tried again to pry the door open, cracking the branch in half in the process. Seeing as there appeared to be no latch, only an edge of damp timber that bulged out slightly from the concrete, the task seemed almost impossible. But I was stubborn. I kept at it. Tearing away a little more soil with my now filthy fingers, pushing and pulling on the door again, then repeating the cycle.

I should have given up. Who knows how long I spent, but finally, as much to my surprise as anything, it moved. Just a little at first, but I was so excited I doubled my efforts, and finally had it open wide enough so I could see inside. At least partially. There wasn't much light down here in the shade of the trees, and this was essentially a black pit. It smelled of mildew and decay too. I could make out a few steps descending into the depths, a small patch of concrete floor below, and all beyond just a black void. Leaving the entrance for a moment, I scaled back up the pile of pine needles and dirt, grabbed a longer stick, and climbed back down. I leaned into the opening, and used the stick to feel around. I was right, it seemed to be just a few stairs, with a fairly flat bottom below. Stick in hand, I squeezed around the door, and crawled inside.

It was cool, cooler than outside, the dank and grimy smell stifling now. I squinted and stared intently but couldn't make out much. It looked like a barren chamber, all concrete and dirt, nothing of interest. The far corner on the left was illuminated by a shaft of light from the door and looked like just a boring stretch of concrete blocks. I couldn't see the right corner clearly, it was buried in shadow and black as night, but I assumed it was the same. Nothing here and I'd wasted my whole afternoon finding that out. I should have known better. A cold gust caught me from that hidden corner, and I recoiled slightly.

Was there a break in the wall there?

I strained my eyes but still couldn't see. The hackles on the back of my neck had started to rise again. I was giving myself the willies. I should get out of here. I climbed back up the steps, walking backwards and staring intently for any movement in the blackness. But there was nothing. I was just scaring myself. The tip of my hand reached the door, and I started to pull myself back out into the afternoon daylight, when something gurgled, and I froze. My skin was ice-cold, my body hairs were standing straight up, and my face was frozen in a mask of fear. Something glimmered in that darkened recess. Something moist and alive.

"Darrin..."

That was my name! How did whatever that was know my name! Sweat rolled down my temples and I froze.

"You've come back Darrin..."

I didn't...didn't know what to say. I spun around, flew up the steps, ripped the skin on my shoulder squeezing out the door, and tried to scamper out of the gully. Only the detritus slid out from under me and I fell flat on my face. Tears streamed down my cheeks, snot dribbled from my nose, and I dug furiously, convinced that any minute now that thing would grab me from behind.

It didn't, I made it out of the hole and ran as fast as I could through the woods.

They seemed endless, the manicured back yards of civilization nowhere in site. My legs burned, I stumbled and almost fell countless times, my knees and ankles constantly twisted into painful contortions and I struggled to stay upright.

Finally erupting out into a backyard, the carpet of pine needles gave way to a swath of damp grass. I darted past a swing set, alongside a duplex, and out into a neighborhood street. Glancing around, I could make out the court by my house, and headed for it. The warm, dusty air of suburbia had replaced the smothering detritus of the woods, and the late afternoon sun beat down on my heaving skin.

Everything seemed almost normal again. Almost silly. I slumped in exhaustion and tromped down the road back home.

The Next Morning

I woke in my bed. It was a bunk bed the lower level occupied by my brother when he was younger, but now he had his own room and his own bed. Funny, I couldn't remember what day it was. The room was warm and well lit, so it must be mid-morning. If it was that late, it must also be the weekend. I was still in my one-piece pale blue pajamas and felt well rested. I wondered what time it was. If it was the weekend, surely my mom would be in the downstairs kitchen, making breakfast. I climbed down from the top bunk, gingerly opened the door, and stepped out.

Damn it was bright in here. I must really have slept in. I rounded the stairway and sauntered downstairs. Turning the corner, I saw a stool pulled up to the kitchen counter. A plate with eggs, bacon, and toast rested on it, a glass of orange juice just beside.

Was this for me?

I didn't see anyone else around. Ambling over, I mounted the stool, glanced around again at the apparently empty kitchen, and dug in. The food was still warm, the OJ still cool, none of this could be that old. *Where did everyone go?*

I wolfed it all down and felt full.

If this was a weekend, why wasn't my brother watching cartoons or playing video games in the living room?

Maybe I was missing something.

Maybe I'd woken up late and there was some event they'd all left early for?

I heard the front door unlock and wondered who it was and if I was in trouble. I heard several voices. The stern, no nonsense tone of my dad, the higher-pitched and annoying prattle of my mother, and what sounded like a deeper, very serious voice. Like some form of authority.

Maybe military police? Or at least someone else in an official capacity.

Rounding the staircase and stepping into view, it was a military policeman. They all formed a trio. My mom maintained her usual, Betty Ford's dumber sister look. My dad appeared as stern and severe as usual, his sharp eyes burrowing into me with condescension, but the MP was in full official garb. Tan uniform, black shiny helmet, and unmistakable black armband with the letters "MP" printed on it.

Without a look of emotion on his face, my dad pointed at me.

"That's him."

The MP drew closer, bent over slightly, and half-asked, half-confirmed my name.

"Darrin?"

"Uh...yeah?"

He straightened up.

"Thanks for watching him. I'll take it from here."

I glanced over at my parents, but they wouldn't even look me in the eye. I felt a sharp pain in my arm, and when I turned, the MP had jabbed a needle into my arm. I started to say something, but blackness enveloped me just as I opened my mouth.

Rise and Shine

I emerged from a deep sleep. It was a great sleep actually. I felt well rested, with a renewed sense of vim and vigor. Yawning, the skin on my face pulled tight, and I noticed the back of my head felt a little raw. Like a cut or something. I didn't remember scraping it. Maybe with how quickly I left the woods... I was pretty on edge last night. Strange, none of that was in my dreams. I don't even recall what it was, just that something had me worked up. I went to raise my hand but it only went halfway before abruptly stopping. I looked over in surprise and noticed that leather bands encircled my wrists, a steel chain securing the bracelets to metal guardrails on the bed. Wait, my ankles felt restrained as well!

I sat up. This wasn't my bed at all! I was on some mobile gurney, like in a hospital. I looked around in shock.

Stained concrete walls boxed me in, high black counters rising up to eye level and covered with a strange mix of metal equipment. Tubular gear with brass parts and a few test tubes.

Where the fuck was I?

I tried looking straight up and was quickly blinded. As I ducked my head down a fuzzy orange pattern burned into my retina. My head itched even more now, and had even started to hurt. I heard a nearby door clicking open. Quickly laying back down, I closed my eyes and pretended I was asleep. Maybe I'd catch some random comment that would help explain what the fuck was going on. I could hear footsteps, and one sounded heavier than the other. The scent of detergent and the oil my dad put on his guns hit me, and I noticed there hadn't really ever been a scent in the room before.

"Was there much trouble extracting him?"

"No sir, the parents knew where they stood."

"He's been with them since he was a newborn, right?"

"Yes sir."

I heard something else enter the room. The footsteps were soft, but they dragged unnaturally, as if whoever it was had a limp. A kind of fetid odor wafted in as well, the brininess of it stinging my nose. I suppressed an urge to crinkle it and tried to maintain my illusion of sleep.

"Soooo. Problems I see?"

The voice sounded guttural and strange, accompanied by a wet slur.

"We think this is the first time. Nothing to be alarmed at."

"That's what they all say when they screw up. Did you take care of it?"

"Quickly. A little brain surgery and he's ready for another transplant."

"You think that was necessary?"

"Only sure way to get rid of the memories."

The voice sounded even more odd as it drew closer. Like foreign or something.

"Perhaps we should just terminate this one?"

"Oh no, you know how long they take to grow. Otherwise he's tested well. It should all still be fine. We'll just restart him with a new family."

Brain surgery! Did they mean me? Oh god, is that why my head hurts?

My eyes popped wide open, and I sprang up as much as I could, the restraints pulling my arms as they painfully twisted my shoulders.

There was a military guy, a full-on olive officers uniform that was decorated with badges, an old scientist looking guy beside him. Face mask, white lab coat, gray hair, all par for the course.

But that third thing beside them... Oh God. Was this for real?

The things flesh was yellow and glistening. Beady, black eyes peered out from deep-set groves, its mouth a gaping hole of spindly teeth. The arms terminated in a writhing mass of tentacles. And a smell...like raw sewage...

"I thought you had it sedated?"

"We did. Must have a high tolerance."

I felt a prick on my arm and turned just in time to see that scientist-looking guy poking me with a needle.

Everything went black.

Home Sweet Home

"Arron, son, you feeling alright?"

"Yeah dad. I know we are going to Six Flags today. I just had the weirdest dream. One of those ones where it almost feels real."

Dad looked skeptical.

"What was it about?"

"Oh, I can never remember my dreams."

"Maybe it's all that sci-fi you watch. Mother says it rots your brain."

"Yes Dad. No it doesn't dad, I'll be down in a moment."

"Get up now. If you're not dressed and downstairs in 10 minutes, we are leaving you behind."

"Yes Dad."

I rolled over and looked at the Batman poster that stared at me from the opposite wall. He was always a favorite of mine.

WATCHING THE WORLD BURN

THE STORM

The sky was engulfed in a cat and dog downpour. I was sure I was lost, and this old station wagon was sliding all over the road. Not that I could even tell where the road was. The engine leaked oil, and smoke was trickling out of the vents in a hazy fog. I tried rolling down the window, but it barely helped. The musty smell was instantly replaced by a damp spring aroma. Only now with the bonus of rain pelting me. I tried to hold the wheel with one outstretched arm, as I reached out to roll up the window. The wheel slipped and the car slid. As I over-corrected in panic, the vehicle glided sideways, and I slid towards a wall of trees. The gloom miraculously parted and I missed the trunks as I was delivered into a well-lit lot. Every muscle tense, the vehicle ground to a halt.

Gasping for air, my fingers lost color gripping the wheel. Splaying them out, I slowly retracted and shook my hand. Even though it didn't look like an actual parking space, death had come close and I was too rattled to think clearly. I cracked the door open and made a dash for the distant shadows.

A few galloping strides later, and I tripped onto a sidewalk. Stumbling over the curb, I skidded across a concrete wall and cried out in pain. Ducking under the canopy, torrents of rainwater poured inches from my face. Swallowing air, I tried to catch my breath. My palms burned, strands of my mo-hawk clung to my face and I shivered as I attempted to shake some of the water off. Grasping the bottom of my Misfits t-shirt, I balled the cloth up and wrung it out. Water splashed across the pavement, but the garment looked no drier. Trying to fight off how cold I was, I glanced around in desperation. The downpour hadn't let up, but the scent hitting my nostrils seemed softer and more welcoming. It was moist and harbored the bite of early spring. Turning back to the wall, I could see a plate glass window and what looked like a door just beyond. *Funny, I didn't recall that.* I was such a mess that I debated for a moment whether it would be rude to go in. I decided that anything was better than freezing. I walked up and peered in. White lettering, buried under a sheen of dust, advertised "books". Beyond the glass, dark forms were all I could make out. I tried to peer in, but the reflections of the storm made it useless. Pulling off my boots, I poured water out and opened the door.

INSIDE

The brightness of daylight faded almost immediately. Glares of the previous brilliance danced in my vision as I attempted to adjust. Warm spots of illumination glowed on my sides. Lamps I supposed. The blurred image of what resembled a desk lay beyond. I squeezed my eyes closed, re-opening them and trying to focus. An old lady sat behind the desk, her brown hair devolving into ratty white strands. What she was seated behind resembled more of a Victorian relic than anything of this era. She was lost in some book. and I tried to make as little noise as possible as I shuffled past.

The dusky smell of old paper and wood overtook the watery abyss I had just left. I was almost to the first row of shelves when a raspy whisper caught my ear.

"Darron?"

The appellation was barely audible, the only other sound the steady drum of the storm, and a cold sensation crawled up my spine. Hesitating a moment, I turned and tried to put up a nonchalant pretense.

"You know me?"

Still buried in her book, I had second thoughts that she had even spoken at all. As I turned back towards the mountains of books, she spoke again.

"It was only a matter of time."

Pausing, I noticed that she refused to look at me as I walked back. The old rug I crossed possessed the strangest of markings, rune-looking images that were splayed out in circular patterns. Their black shapes were buried in a deluge of geometric patterns. A strong feeling of Deja-Vu washed over. As I closed in on the desk, she turned to face me. Licking her lips with a tongue that seemed way too long, the edges of her mouth peeled back in a labyrinth of wrinkles, dark red stains marring the edges. I stuttered as I approached.

"Did...did you call me?"

Staring now, her pale eyes ever creepier, I could see that the irises looked off. Her jaw moved slowly, the whole side of her face shifting with it. She was hunched over some hidden treasure and as I approached, her right hand ascended. She took a bite, the skin on her face rising and sinking in spots where it shouldn't.

"My name? Did you call my name?"

How did she even know my name?

Another step forward, and I was bombarded with a horrible smell. In a low voice, she croaked as I stepped forward.

"I should have killed you long ago."

My line of sight zeroed in on what she was hunched over and nausea washed over.

It was a child! That smell...intestines and gore.

My nose screwed up, I doubled over and started to retch. She cackled.

"Did you really forget?"

My outstretched hand was all that saved me as I fell. Dust kicked up as I hit the rug, throwing me into a frenzy of racking sneezes. I was allergic to almost everything as a kid, and this seemed way too familiar. Gasping and wheezing while the grownups around me laughed and joked. They didn't seem to care, and I hated them. Hated them all.

"You've been among the normal people so long Darron."

She drew it out, the last portion almost a slur.

"You've forgotten what you truly are. Such a delicious little morsel you were. It was cruelty! Look but don't touch!"

Then, in the blink of an eye, she was looming over me. I realized that her eyes were never pale. They were black.

Black as coal. And her mouth! Her mouth was impossibly large. A bloody chasm that was host to rows upon rows of spindly teeth.

She cackled, and looking for all

the world like an old woman again, settled back on her haunches.

"Ha-ha...such a weak thing. It's long past the time when I can have my way with you."

I wanted to say something, but what? Worse still, I had this terrible sense of Deja vu. I tried to dredge up details, but nothing was forthcoming.

"What...what do you want?"

She, and I was beginning to wonder if it was a she at all, shrugged her shoulders.

"I just want to watch the world burn. And you're the start. "

I sprang forward. The dust of the carpet puffed about me, clogging my lungs and assaulting my eyes as my shoulder impacted the glass and I spilled out into the light of day.

THE THING THAT NEVER WAS

Even though blinding sunlight assaulted me, the empty lot was still a wondrous site. I gulped in air, the dampness of spring a bath of freshness. Swallowing breaths of pine and oak, I could see that my station wagon sat off to the far left. It looked forlorn, alone in a swath of sun-bleached asphalt. Cracks and potholes speckled the pavement, broken tree limbs and sodden masses of leaves fighting for space amid craters of decay. Some of that must be remnants from the storm. I turned to look back. Maybe the bookstore would all be almost comical in the light of day.

The remnants of some decrepit strip mall edged the lot. Its two remaining panes of glass dusky portals into empty darkness. Twin doors sided the windows, one hosting the demarcation "Books". I wondered if I should wander back for a closer view, but the horror of my recent experience was still fresh. The last thing I wanted was to poke a sleeping bear. The sooner I was in my car, the better. I needed to get back on the road and back out on familiar streets. My head felt thick and clogged, maybe that would clear it out.

I quickened my pace into a jog as I closed in on my car. Sweat built up in my armpits, my damp socks now warm and tight. My head swam, the recent events rolling over me in waves of disbelief. Something rattled in the distance, but I didn't dare look. I was almost in the car. Once inside, I could turn around and see that it was nothing. Another rattle was followed by yet another. I picked up the pace. Something thudded behind me. Something heavy.

Just a few seconds and I would be in the car.

I could almost touch the door...in fact I was inches from it... when the sky fell.

HELL HAS NO FURY...

Thunder blew out my eardrums as I flew face-first onto the pavement. The asphalt was way too hard, snapping my arm as I landed. Pain like nothing I had ever experienced shot through and I howled into the void, my eyes welling with tears. I tried to roll to my left, the act of turning still another stab of pain. I realized my second arm bone had cracked and was now snapping. I screamed as I doubled into a fetal ball. My eyelids crusted together, and my sense of reality grew foggy. Through narrow slits, I could see that where my car used to be there was now a glowing pit. I blinked, my head felt underwater, and reality slipped by the moment. Something flitted across my field of vision and I looked up as I rolled over. What appeared to be hailstones were falling out of the sky. One slammed into the lot and fire spewed from it, the nearby leaves reduced to ash. Smoke sped towards me in a writhing wall. Flying detritus stung my face as the wind besieged my shattered limbs. I tried to double over, but the gale was too strong. My vision blurred again and I could feel my grip on consciousness slipping. Then all went black.

IT ONLY GETS WORSE FROM HERE

Such strange dreams. I was five, sprawled out on the top mattress of my bunk bed. Something was missing and I kept groping around for it. Finally, I grabbed the flashlight under my pillow, my shield against the terrors of the dark, and scanned the room.

I investigated the wrinkled covers in the lower bunk. Nothing except for my sleeping little brother. I scooted to the edge, and climbed down, my hands gripping tightly on the wooden rails. Dropping to the floor, I ventured out into the hall, flashlight still at the ready.

That was strange. I didn't remember all these bookshelves in the entrance hall. In fact, the whole scene appeared to be altering before my eyes. The hall widened and the shelves elongated and as I neared them. I tried to turn tail, only my loose pajamas twisted, and I tripped. Into a rug that I never remembered crossing. The landing kicked up clouds of dust, and I doubled over in hacking fits. As snot poured down my upper lip, I tried to move, but my arms seemed to be made of lead.

Something was emerging from the nearby stairwell. As it's shadow grew larger, I clinched my eyes, snorting and hacking feverishly.

Then, it was upon me. I cracked open my eyes to a vision of a giant, fish-like eye. Tenacles slithered in and out of my periphery vision. Then, the voice of that old lady from the bookstore broke out.

Wait, *I hadn't met her yet!*

I snapped awake. I was on the same pavement as before, only now it was pitted in an even more extensive labyrinth of craters. I could hear again, and my arm didn't sting. I took a couple of deep breaths, savoring a thick brew of sulfur and pulverized stone. Glancing at my arm, I saw that the healed flesh was now contorted and textured like that of a burn victim. I twisted to look closer and realized that although the ass of my jeans was shredded, my skin was no longer raw. Pulling in my feet, I slowly rose.

My car was now a molten mass of embers. I looked back at the strip mall. Whatever had fallen from the sky had eviscerated it as well. Remnants of a few walls remained, the rest only a tangle of ash and ruin. Some motion in the sky grabbed my attention again and as I watched, the very fabric of the air seemed to double in upon itself. It tore open and expelled one of the creatures from my nightmare. A moment later, a smaller beast with more legs fell to earth. The opening folded, leaving a pungent scent in its wake. The glare of midday broke in, burning away the remnants of storm clouds. Stuffing my hands in my pockets, I headed towards the edge of the lot. All was silent and eerie now, with only the gale of the wind and rustle of the leaves showing any life.

Turning left once I hit the curb, I trudged down an empty roadway. The trees cast long stripes of shadows over an asphalt riddled with smoking craters. My head seemed unusually thick and I shivered despite the warmth of the day.

Was the bookstore just a crazy dream?

I recalled all the weird family interactions I'd had over the years. Aunts, uncles, grandparents, they were strangers, peripheral ties that popped into and out of my life. But they all had this pretense they were blood. It seemed arbitrary. They barely made eye contact and only uttered the perfunctory cues.

Was that a real thing or just normal teenage angst?

As I rounded the corner, I could see the tail end of a battered old car. Apparently, it had skidded off the road and into a tree. Probably in the recent storm. I couldn't see how mangled the front was from this angle, but the driver's side door hung open. As I drew closer, a throaty gurgle resounded, followed by the eruption of a bloodied, bare arm. The fingers were splayed, desperately reaching for the pavement. A moment later, a blonde, middle-aged woman, sweat shimmering on her blood-stained neck, crawled out. She rolled onto the concrete in a spectacular failure of an exit, scraping her exposed knees as she tumbled across the pavement. Scrambling to her feet, blood marring her tank top and shorts, she cried out-

"Angie? Angie! Angie!"

Turning back to the car, she tore at the handle of the dented door. When it popped open, she desperately clawed for something, tossing useless strands of cloth across the road.

"Baby! Baby! You'll be alright!"

She emerged; arms wrapped around a crying baby girl.

"Mommy's here. It's OK, It's OK."

In a motion that almost seemed surreal, one of those giant creatures broke out of the woods, hurdled the car, scooped up the child, and was already disappearing in the trees on the other side. The lady screamed; her features impossibly drawn out as she spurted gibberish. Tears streamed down her face, and she bounded after her baby girl.

I wondered what was wrong with me. This whole thing should be at least a bit disturbing, but it didn't affect me at all. I halfheartedly tried but still couldn't bring myself to feel anything. Anything at all. Looking down at my disfigured arm, I shrugged and kept walking.

THE HORROR...OH THE HORROR

Blood and Snow

It's cold... so cold. I can't feel my fingers anymore. Wet and salty, a string of blood descends from my nose, curling down my lip and springing free in a final, fatal plunge. I struggle to catch my breath and stare up at the blinding sky.

Cottony wisps of clouds tumble in a mad roll through the pale blue. I try to drop my gaze but can't. The brilliant sheen of the snow assaults me like some living Arctic creature. I'm going to die out here. Maybe it's better that way. I won't have to see the doom, the horror that I've brought.

I cough, a dry hacking that only pulls more of the frigid air into my aching lungs. Rising to my feet, I stumble forward through the snow, my path accompanied by a trail of crimson.

And It All Started So Nicely

I made the connection at London/Heathrow airport. Never one of my favorites, with all its mad bustle and confusion. Wandering through the corridors in a sleep-deprived haze, I struggled to locate and read the monitors for connecting flights. As I sheepishly lugged my bag up the gleaming tiled halls travelers loomed in and out of my peripheral vision. Maybe it was just me, but they all seemed angry—no, not quite angry, more annoyed and aloof. They were all slimmer, more fashionably dressed, and definitely more predatory than I was used to in America.

Maybe my perspective was just warped by jetlag and the six-hour time change, but my head filled with images of all the horrible things that had happened over the centuries in Europe. The tortures. The inquisitions. The class cruelty and inevitable retaliation by the masses. I saw what I believed was a hint of that on their faces. Not on the surface, more of a buried, subtle influence. But like I said, maybe it was just jetlag.

I grabbed a coffee, put my whole two-pound bill on a credit card, found my flight to Glasgow, and dropped down on one of the hard, gleaming metal seats. My back was killing me, and I kept starting to doze off, only to be woken a minute later by the uncomfortable seat. I had almost made it to dreamland when they announced boarding. The flight would be so short there was little point in going back to sleep. Besides, I was keyed up. In a restless, numb sort of way.

A short hop, and I was descending through the clouds, stone hamlets and bright green fields sprawling out beneath. A gut-shaking drop onto the landing strip, and we eased up to the gate. Rubbing my eyes, I tried to will away some of the jetlag. The passengers clamored to their feet and slowly trucked off the plane, passing by the way-too-cheerful stewardess welcoming us to Scotland.

This was a much nicer, more manageable airport, and a short taxi ride later, and I was on a train to Edinburgh and the start of my vacation.

Rolling hills of grass flew past, the vibrant green speckled with wiry patches of yellow weeds. Small white dots, the telltale marks of sheep, marbled the fields. Sporadic houses dappled the landscape as well, their stone facades colored with a green patina of moss. They looked as if they had been there as long as the hills. I dozed off in the early morning light, my head nestled against the window.

"Edinburgh."

The announcement woke me up, and half-dazed, I grabbed the handle of my canvas bag and wandered out onto the concrete platform. Jaunting up the steps, I passed locals who glanced at me as if annoyed by my very presence. Another taxi ride, this time by a young, fashionably dressed driver, listening to some mind-numbing electronica, and I arrived at the city center. The streets remained cobblestone, but the edges of the buildings grew a bit sharper and more modern looking as we pulled up.

The Ibis Hotel line never failed to give me the simplest of accommodations. A bed that was almost too thin and stiff to qualify as a bed, a particleboard desk, and a TV much smaller than the one I had at home. Good thing I wasn't expecting any local atmosphere. Dropping my belongings on the bedspread, I was off to explore.

The city really was a sharp-looking place, filled with majestic Gothic architecture. Dark gray slabs of stone wrapped the sides, the path narrow cobblestone streets. The facades of the buildings were weathered and stained with age and centuries of soot. Fuzzy green moss assailed the walls and tree trunks like some unstoppable affliction. I wandered up the Royal Mile, one of the oldest streets in the city, and polluted by one too many tourist traps selling trinkets, kilts, maps, cashmere... anything they thought the rubes would buy. The city was built on another city, and some tours offered an underground "City of the Dead" tour. The narrators spun fantastic tales about the residents of the vaults. Plague victims, poor immigrants, and young unwed mothers kicked out of wealthy households for fear of social rejection. Scheming harpies would take them in, reassure them that they and their child would find safe haven, and then slit their throats if they lived through childbirth. Most didn't, they died in childbirth. Once born, the children, if fit enough, would be sold to wealthy families. The conditions were so horrible, raw feces often dripped down the walls. Rats were ubiquitous, and archeologists found evidence that they were skewered and roasted for food. The average life expectancy there was only three to eight months. On a lighter note, one tour agency offered a trip up to Loch Ness and I couldn't pass on that!

They say there is a ruined castle up there and offer boat tours across the Loch. Even though I had very little hope of actually seeing Nessie, it was on my list of places to visit.

Thirty-eight pounds later, and I had a ticket for an 8:00 AM bus ride leaving the next morning. Popping into a local pub for a quick Guinness and some food, I headed to bed early, taking a sleeping pill to dull the anticipation.

EMBARKING ON A LITTLE TRIP

Wandering down for the morning tour, outfitted in my brown leathers—coat, pants, and boots (it's pretty cold in Scotland in the winter)—and twisting my newsboy cap on straight, I joined the crowd of about twenty gathered outside the travel agency. I double-checked my pockets, just to make sure I had my little mag light and digital camera.

I was barely awake, but the other travelers seemed a bit more upbeat, conversing in various exotic tongues. I took second row behind a family of noisy Italians, and leaned back to relax, hoping to catch a little shuteye. A prim older woman, well dressed in a navy-blue short skirt and jacket, climbed the steps to greet us. Taking a front seat behind the driver, she seemed genuinely cheerful as she recounted the highlights of the trip, which included a journey up the Scottish Highlands as much as the destination itself.

Rumbling off through the city, we were soon headed into the foothills of northern Scotland. The stories were fascinating, tales of mass slaughter, tyranny, and the constant betrayal of the smarmy upper class. The family in front of me, despite the fact that they probably saw each other the entire rest of the year, felt the need to talk incessantly over the tour guide. I held my finger to my lips and whispered for them to be quiet, but they either ignored me or didn't understand and droned on. A pair of lesbians sat to my right. Both were young, one a cute slim brunette, the other more mannish and stouter. They would alternate between looking in opposite directions, like they were not together, and being all over each other.

As we passed flowing hills of heather and trees, fronting lochs and snow-capped mountains, the cute girl would spring forward. Positioning her Cannon Rebel just right, its massive lens just inches from my face, she would assume a serious pose, sprawl out in a stable position, and snap pictures of the passing landscape. She didn't seem to notice me or didn't care.

I was falling asleep again. It didn't help that it was warm in the bus, and I was dressed in heavy winter clothing. I started to doze off, snapping out of it as we pulled up to our first rest stop. Mulling off to the left were the strangest looking cattle I'd ever seen. Stringy burnt orange hair hung in thick tufts from their heavyset bodies. They reminded me of rebellious metal-heads, in a Wayne's World sort of way. Thin-sliced meat of unknown origin and white cheese, sandwiched between rolls of bleached white bread, was all the restaurant offered. Well, that's not entirely true. They also had some very suspicious looking soup. At least the soup had a hint of vegetables in it, something the sandwiches obviously lacked. England's not exactly known for its food, and apparently that reputation extends up into Scotland as well. At least the tourist trap areas of Scotland. The coffee at least was good, if twice the price and half the size of a U.S. coffee. The store attached to the restaurant was obviously also geared to tourists, and contained everything from stuffed Nessie dolls to an endless variety of everything Hollywood expects of the Scots. Kilts, hats, mugs, and pictures with just the right lighting and perspective to be the sort of thing that neither offends nor inspires anyone.

I climbed back onto the bus, hoping the final destination held more authenticity than what I'd seen so far. I had almost dozed off again when we pulled up into the dirt lot of Loch Ness.

A sprawling, ranch-style dwelling greeted us. It looked to be of recent construction, its large glass windows framed by freshly painted planks of wood. Inside, the shop spread out a bit, with a store, a cafe, a small movie theater, and thanks to the embankment it was built on, a wide-open downstairs. Giant two-story glass windows opened out onto a vision of a ruined castle, although I wouldn't have known it was a castle if the tour guide hadn't told us. It looked more like a fort, and the broken-down remnants of one at that.

I headed to the café first. Another quick coffee, to get the last of the cobwebs out of my head, and I wandered down the steps and out the back door. The grass was intensely green. Shorter and lusher than what I was used to seeing in America, it spread out in a small procession of hills and valleys. I wandered down the curving concrete path that burrowed through, feeling a little lightheaded. I passed the remains of a giant, centuries old catapult, now a monument with its own descriptive placard, and behind it was a winding path that led up into the ruins. Not much to see, really. So far, this trip has not lived up to my expectations. You've seen one ruined castle; you've seen them all. Tiny, cramped quarters, and a narrow, steep stairway that now sported a handrail. The crumbling stone walls looked entirely out of place with the shiny modern addition.

A boat was pulling up at the nearby dock, and our tour guide warned us that if we missed the boat, we would be stranded a good four hours from Edinburgh.

I wandered down, a couple of young kids in pastel clothing yelling at each other as they passed. Their overweight father followed, yelling at what I assumed was his wife. Dumpy and middle aged, her chin receded down into her neck. She shrugged her shoulders in exasperation. Real sense of authentic Scottish atmosphere I was experiencing.

LOCH NESS

The boat reminded me of the ferries we had back in the states. Minus the wide lower level that holds the cars, but with the same industrial appearance. You entered the rear, climbed up a metal staircase to the second floor, and were greeted by an austere bar. A few bolted down tables formed neat rows, and waitresses who looked like they hated their job reluctantly helped the customers. Just past the dining room was a further set of stairs that ascended to the roof. I headed up those and wandered out into the bright sunlight. Grated benches circled the perimeter, another row down the center. Almost all were taken by noisy, brightly colored tourists. I found a spot at the rear and settled in.

Gusts of water sprayed us, and the announcer droned on about some well-known racing figure, decades ago, that tried to set a water speed record and died in the attempt. Funny. For a place of such intrigue, it seemed most of the locals were treating the more fantastical legends like a fairy tale. Like it was an embarrassment and barely worth mentioning.

The Loch is a giant body of water, threaded throughout by underwater caves, and most likely was at some point open to the sea. There have been so many sightings of something strange, it was a bit like UFOs in my book. You couldn't rely on any one report, but taken together, and considering the number of reputable witnesses, it became pretty clear that something was going on.

As we crossed the loch, the sky darkened a little when rolling clouds passed under the sun. It was already a bit cold, what with the open breeze coming off the water, and this only made it worse. The whole of Scotland is constantly bombarded by strong winds, and the farther north we got, the harsher they seemed to become.

The spray picked up. Good thing I was wearing a leather jacket, as a thin sheen of mist now coated everything. The announcer kept droning on about William of Orange. She followed this with a harangue about Richard the Lionhearted and the real reason he was so named being something about how his heart was kept after his death for sacred burial. A bank of fog rolled in, veiling the tree-lined banks. The wind picked up as well, so formidable now it almost tore my hat off. I grabbed it just in time and buttoned up my coat. The temperature seemed to be dropping, and I pulled out my gloves as well.

A few of the tourists headed downstairs, to the relative warmth of the indoor bar. It looked far to cut and paste for me, and besides, I didn't come this far to settle for overpriced drinks in some gloomy excuse for a bar.

I glanced around and noticed that only a few other people remained up here. A young couple was seated nearby. Both were uber white, with matching jeans and gray sweatshirts pulled over their lanky bodies. On the far side sat an old man. He must have been at least seventy, the brim of his hat pulled down over his liver-spotted features. He gazed serenely out at the water, his hands buried in the pockets of his waistcoat, and seemed unmovable, as if he were a permanent fixture of the ship.

Just my luck, the annoying family from the castle was still here, tucked in the far corner near the small cabin. The man was berating his wife over something, and she was looking off in the opposite direction, doing her best to ignore him. A hand tapped me on the shoulder.

"Sir, the captain has requested that everyone come below deck."

It was a ship's mate; one I apparently hadn't seen before. He sported a young face, but something implied he was much older.

"Sir, it's not really a request. Everyone needs to come below."

"What's going on?"

"Nothing, just some inclement weather."

The boat pitched, and the man lost his footing, stumbling back and catching the guardrail at the last minute. A low laugh resonated, and I looked for the source. The old man, eyes slit as small as marbles, was grinning. For the first time I noticed that a long scar ran down his cheek. I glanced back but the German couple was gone. In fact, everyone was gone. A gust of water pelted me and just as I stumbled forward, I lost my balance. Glancing down at my hands, I saw that some dark, sticky fluid was trailing off them. I spun around and the headless body of the ship's mate, neck jugulars still spurting out a crimson fountain, toppled overboard.

"You know... we're all going to die here."

I twirled back around. The old man was closer now and chuckling softly. The floor shifted violently under my body, throwing me against the outer railing. Something had rammed the boat, and I could hear it taking on water. I looked back, but the old man had disappeared.

Did he go over the side?

The deck had tilted toward me. I should have seen him. The wind had become a deafening gale, but I could still make out muffled shouts below. The deck was declining at an ever-steeper angle. I inched to the other side and looked down. Below a stout looking man, probably the captain, was surrounded by a few crewmen who were hurriedly putting a boat in the water. Just a Spartan rowboat, their forms almost silhouettes under the roiling mist, but they gave me the impression that they were desperately trying to abandon ship.

"Hey!"

I yelled at them repeatedly, my voice growing hoarse, but they didn't respond. I turned and half-ran, half-slid down the deck. Ducking into the stairwell, I noticed for the first time how dramatically the ship had tilted. The stairs were now at a steep angle and a thick, warm smell wafted out of the bowels.

I crawled down, grasping the rail and stumbling clumsily. The smell intensified as I reached the bottom. The lights were off, a pale blue sifting in through the windows, and I couldn't hear any voices. Dark lumps were strewn across the floor down here, making the bowels a maze. I stepped forward, and something tacky gripped the soles of my shoes. With a groan, the ship tilted more. I brushed the floor and lifted my fingers. A sheen of blood coated the fingertips. Sunlight broke through the windows, and I could now see what littered the floor.

It was the entire crew! All those tourists!

Fuck!

Half-stumbling, half-climbing, and using the edges of the tables as anchors, I squirmed through the carnage, a sickening crunch greeting me every time I stepped on a body. Panic was rising in my throat, the room growing fouler, and I fought back the urge to wretch.

A harrowing five tables, and I made it across. Quickly muscling down the slope of a stairway I reached the ground floor. The ship was tilting badly now, and as I twisted, trying to get a firm footing on the deck, I slid.

Tumbling down in a flurry of flapping leather, leaving behind a trail of bloody smears, I smashed into the guardrail. Struggling to my feet, I glanced over the edge.

The rowboat was still there, oars and all, but there was no sign of the crew. Ducking under the bars and dangling from the ship's edge, I eased myself down into the rowboat. Grasping the oars, I started paddling vigorously.

The wind cut across my face, and as I launched out from the cover of the boat, it grew stronger. A gust caught my hat, and it sailed off into oblivion. I kept paddling, glancing back at the now receding shadow of a sinking ship.

DRY LAND

I don't know how long I lay there, bent over on the beachhead, coughing and shaking. The rowboat was beached, and I had managed to crawl up to the wood line.

The ship was long gone, the loch returned to a placid body of water. The sky had cleared a little, the dark clouds metamorphosing into a calmer slate gray. A thin black crust was flaking off my fingers, and I rubbed them against the sides of my coat. Standing upright and looking around, I felt utterly alone and abandoned. I hadn't felt it this intensely since I was a little kid, lost in the woods. Funny, the memories that flood you at odd times.

I listened keenly, straining for any noise that sounded out of place. Nothing but the whipping of the pine branches.

Higher ground seemed safer, and I started climbing up the slope.

IN THE WOODS

The wind bit into my face as I climbed. The pines dwindled into stubby trees, their short branches and squat trunks completely foreign to anything I had back home. Even the grass looked thicker and greener, as it coiled in on itself in dense clusters.

As I climbed, shrubbery broke out, cloistering around my feet in a contorted maze of thorny leaves. Apparently, there was no rest for the weary in this harsh terrain. My ears and nose began to go numb. Sweat built up in my armpits, quickly stiffening in the frigid folds that scoured my arms. I kept climbing, the incline growing steeper as I ascended.

Piles of rock started to sprout up on my left, quickly growing into a steep wall of granite that partially blocked the biting wind. The trail underfoot devolved into a contorted mess of slippery loose stone, and I slowed. More granite took over, scaling up on either side as the path progressed. Snow was beginning to dominate, crusting the clifftops in gleaming caps that launched feathery trails with every draft.

The trail narrowed to a crevice, and I had to turn sideways as I squeezed myself through. I almost got stuck twice, and had to pause, wriggle back and forth, and try again. After a few feet, it widened, letting out onto a small plain. And wonder of wonders, at the far end was a small stone cabin. Its thatched roof was in good enough repair that it looked recently occupied, but a foggy haze obscured all the other details.

Stumbling toward it, my feet slipping through a damp carpet of green, I bent my head as the wind whipped around the mountaintop. I wondered who could live in such environs.

THE CABIN

Eventually the cabin came into focus. I didn't see a window, and the mist was so thick I couldn't tell if there was any light coming from underneath the door. I knocked.

Minutes passed, but there was no response. I knocked again, louder this time. Still nothing. I gave the door a push, but it didn't budge. I pushed again, harder, but still no movement. Backing up, I threw my shoulder in and it gave slightly.

A flickering light was coming from inside. Either someone was home, or they soon would be. I threw myself into it again, and the door creaked open.

I had expected an earthen floor, and some setup out of the Middle Ages, but the interior looked distinctly modern. Simple, but modern. A floor tiled with neatly cut slate. A fairly featureless, but solid oak table, encircled by four chairs. The windows were apparently at the front of the house, their latticed panes crisscrossing the table in alternating lines of shade and light. On the stove, a pot softly whistled. Whoever was staying here would probably be back soon. Beyond the kitchen was a hallway with what looked like a closed door on the right side. It was then I realized how badly I needed to take a leak.

I rounded the counter and slowly opened the door. My eyes had adjusted a bit to the shade, and I ran my fingers up and down the inside wall for a light switch. Then I remembered that all electric outlets and switches in the UK were on the wall outside of the room, and I ran my hand alongside until I bumped into a switch.

More modern looking than the rest of the cabin, the bathroom before me was a tidy, small alcove of gray stone. A narrow toilet and sink shouldered the lip of a miniscule shower stall. I did my business, feeling much relieved, and headed back out. Flicking off the light, I saw that one of the chairs was now occupied. Not only that, but the occupant resembled the old man on the boat.

"And what would you be doing here?"

My mind raced as I tried to come up with an explanation that didn't sound crazy.

"I'm... lost. My boat... I was a tourist, down on Loch Ness. We capsized, I need to call someone, find... a way... out..."

"And just who would you be?"

"I'm sorry, I'm Jon. I stumbled across your house. I knocked, but no one answered..."

"You look kind of funny, Jon. You talk funny, too. You foreign?"

"Yeah, American. Look, I'm sorry, I didn't mean to intrude."

"Yeah, well, you have a funny way of going about it."

He stared at me evenly for an uncomfortable moment.

"But we're God-fearing people. The good book tells us to help those in need, and I guess that would include you."

That last part was left dangling in the air, almost like a question. About my faith. Whether I believed in a god. As if that would determine if I was worth helping. I decided not to answer. The man anchored his hands on the wooden armrests and slowly rose.

"You look cold. Want some tea?"

"Yeah, thanks. You don't by any chance have coffee, do you?"

He laughed a little, twisting in the direction of the stove.

"We don't have any of that here, but I can give you some tea if you like."

"Sounds great."

NEVER TRUST THE DEAD

I woke up curled in a ball on the floor. My mouth was dry and salty, my exposed cheeks and hands freezing. The ambient light was dull and gray, degenerating into an opaque haze as it descended from the windowsill. I struggled to my feet, feeling numb and sore. The clean tile floor was gone, replaced by packed sand. Another cold gust hit, and I realized it was coming from the window. I looked over at it and saw that there was no glass. There wasn't even a frame. The raw stone edges looked untouched, like they hadn't been burdened with a pane in ages. As I spun back around, I saw that there was no table, no stove, just the long-abandoned shell of a room. Pale beams shone down from holes in the thatched roof. Wind rustled the straw, the jagged edges shaking indignantly. I rose to my feet and stumbled toward where I remembered having entered. No doorway existed.

I wandered over to the window and peered out.

The cabin apparently edged a sheer drop down a precipice of granite, the recesses disappearing into a drifting tumult of fog far below.

Was I dreaming? Had I been dreaming before and this was real?

I turned back around and traipsed into the center of the room. The chamber looked archaic, all rugged stone blocks sloppily mortared into the form of walls. As I looked down, I realized that not only was there no layer of sand coating a stone floor, but there also wasn't even a stone floor. The hairs on my neck started to bristle and I suddenly had the odd sense I wasn't alone.

I remembered something I heard years ago, how one of the surest signs of a haunting was the sense of a presence. Reality made no sense anymore, and all the ghost stories I'd heard suddenly seemed more relevant.

The only way out of here appeared to be the dark hallway leading to a bathroom, but now there was something ominous about it that I couldn't quite put my finger on.

The wind whipped like a living thing around the corners. It seemed like the gale was trying to intimidate me. It was working.

I looked around again, took a deep breath, and headed into the corridor.

The darkness almost instantly became suffocating, it's surreal thickness drowning me in an inky sea of tension. The temperature rose a little, and thin rivulets of sweat rolled down the sides of my face. I extended my arm as I walked, desperately feeling for something, for anything. The main room behind me receded all too quickly, it's feeble rectangle of illumination growing as suspicious in my mind as the walkway before me.

Was I venturing off course in the dark?

I glanced behind me, but the blackness was absolute now

Was this worse? Had I abandoned my only safe haven? Was that even a safe haven? Whas this even the small house I entered? Did I imagine the old man? Did I imagine the man on the boat, too?

Questions without answers. Moving seemed slightly better than standing still, so I continued.

A wan, reddish light appeared to indicate a door in the distance, and I fought the urge to bolt toward it. I was still treading carefully over unseen ground, and the last thing I needed was to trip on a rock, or fall into some unseen depression.

It was maddeningly slow, and I would speed up slightly with anticipation, then slow down as terrifying thoughts flitted through my head. The hairs on my neck had never gone down. There was the sense of something ancient and evil in the air. The gurgling, bloody neck of the man on the boat flooded into my memory. It was only for a moment, but my skin broke out in a cold sweat, my stomach knotted into a ball, and I gasped in ragged breaths.

At length the sensation ebbed, I regained a small measure of control, and continued forward.

THE CHAPEL

Slowly the red light grew larger, eventually revealing itself as an archway. Well, the frame of one at least. I didn't see any door, and the walkway curved to the right as it approached. I paused, still shielded by the darkness of the hallway. I was now scared of what I would find.

It took a moment, but fear of the dark trumped fear of the light, and with bated breath, I rounded the corner and passed through the archway.

Spreading out before me was a rough-hewn chamber significantly larger than the previous room. Just like the other, it was more ascending walls of stone blocks and floored by packed dirt. Hundreds of candles lined the bottom of the walls, flowing up and down as they scaled over blocks of stone. Mounds of earthen debris littered the floor. I felt no breeze, but the flames flickered, casting trembling strips of light across the room. In the center was what looked like a stone altar. Its smooth sides narrowed as they ascended, the top edges crowned with spires. As I approached, I could make out what looked like an ancient, leather-bound book sitting atop. It was open, and the thick pages were covered in brown scrawls. The strange script was accompanied by illustrations.

I flipped the page. More illustrations, and more of that same script, all in neat cursive rows. The drawings looked like those of some madman, just ovals heavily crisscrossed by small circular sections. They resembled giant mutated beetles that walked upright. As I flipped through a few more pages, they were accompanied by short, stocky, humanoid figures. All had only three fingers per hand, the faces illustrated with beady eyes and a mass of needle-like teeth. Another creature followed. It's limbs were thick and stump-like, the feet like an elephant's. All the drawings were crude, and I wondered if this was some primitive form of a fairy tale.

As I flipped to the next page, the thick paper creaking with the effort, there was a drawing that resembled some kind of topographical map. A tiny square was marked with an X, lines indicating some kind of drop or elevation beside it that seemed to indicate a lake. In fact, the whole thing looked a bit like the brochure pictures of Loch Ness. There was even a series of lines running along one edge, where that ruin of a castle would be. Maybe the X indicated the building I was in? If so, I might be looking at the key to my way back to civilization again. I closed the book gently and for the first time looked at the cover.

It was a dark, mottled brown, and strangely fuzzy as if it was covered in thick hair. Delving my fingers underneath I pulled it towards me.

Fuck, it was heavy!

Heaving it to my left side, I walked toward what looked like the exit, straining a little with the weight.

As I reached the entrance, I leaned forward and peered into the hallway. It was dark and I couldn't see anything but possibly having a map, at least something that placed me, was a step forward. I shuffled down the corridor.

After a few steps, the walkway curved, a detail I didn't notice until my foot smacked into a wall of stone, and I veered to the left.

The book felt as if it grew heavier by the moment, and I was starting to sweat profusely. My breathing became a bit stuffier, and my thighs felt hot and itchy.

Eventually the hall started to lighten up. A faint illumination glowed from the depths and the blank stone walls came into focus.

The light kept increasing, and within a few feet I could see an opening. I couldn't make out any features—the light pouring through was too intense—but I could smell fresh air. A cool draft wafted in, freezing my sweat into ice.

Within a few more feet I was at the edge of a portal and peering down a mountainside. A sandy path, steep but navigable, twisted down the slope. Weeds swooped in on both sides, trailing down the steep hills and into an open savannah. A strong gust burst in, the unexpected force almost knocking me over, and I realized I must be pretty high up. That explained why there were no trees up here, just patches of heather and weeds.

I wandered down, stumbling a little with the weight of the book. Crosswinds smacked me, buffeting my leather coat and slowing my movement, but I was glad to be free of that place.

After a few feet I glanced back at what was now a small, receding black hole that looked like a cave entrance. Only the edges were a little too straight to be natural. I kept walking.

THE HIGHLANDS

The trail leveled out as it descended, and soon I was tromping through woods. The path continued, now in a little poorer repair, beneath a canopy of pine, their shade cutting the ground into gloomy tones of blueish-gray. I was tired, cold, and just now realizing how hungry I was. It was like I had run a marathon, and then been denied sleep. Stepping off the trail, I crouched down next to a large trunk, opened the book, and flipped through the pages. In the daylight, the writing looked to have more of a dark red tone, the pages thick and leathery to the touch.

Lines of strange writing opened up every third page into some mindboggling illustration.

The lighter, more normal environs, and maybe even a second wind, were all kicking in, and I started to look at things in a different light. This book was probably some obscure religious text, which meant I had made an incredible find! I had never seen anything even remotely like this. I'd be famous! Maybe even rich!

The next page opened onto a map of sorts. The same map I had seen inside, the one showing what I assumed was the loch. If it was, and the contours represented elevations in the terrain, the X indicated my former location, and the dotted line marked the trail I was following. Not far from what I assumed was my present location, was an even bigger mark. It was in the woods, and the dotted line of a different trail led to it.

Should I check it out?

Once I got back to civilization, I doubt I would get the chance. There would be a huge hubbub over the book, investigators would flock out here, and it would all be out of my hands.

I felt a little better. Drained, but capable. Standing up, I wandered down the path.

About twenty minutes later, and I thought I had found it. The contour lines seemed to indicate a hill, and the woods rose into one on my left. The trees opened slightly into what could only be a new trail. I decided to chance it, and ventured off the path, treading through fallen leaves and onto a trail that, if worse came to worst, existed solely in my imagination.

NEVER LEAVE THE TRAIL

I was beginning to doubt this was even a trail, and cursing myself for venturing off what may well have been a good chance to return to civilization. Half an hour had passed, and I grew worried that I wouldn't be able to make it back to the path I left.

Stupid! Stupid! Stupid! I couldn't leave well enough alone, I had to go and be the explorer!

I stopped and looked around. This definitely wasn't a path. I had no idea where I was in the woods, no working phone, and if I died out here, it would be no one's fault but my own. Then I noticed that the trees just ahead of me opened up into a small meadow and I wandered towards it, more out of resignation than anything.

The mound of rock in the center of the meadow was a little weird. Large boulders shouldered the sides, a flat chunk of granite gracing the top. A single, scraggly tree, little more than a sapling, wriggled up from the apex. Its roots, however, were huge and monstrous, swarming in a mass of organic cables down the moss-covered sides. At the base of the mound was a large hole. Curiosity getting the best of me, I wandered over, and peered in.

I could make out nothing inside and wondered how deep it was. A shiver passed through me, accompanied by that weird sense that something I couldn't see was there. The feeling grew so intense I spun around and shouted-

"Who's there!"

But there was no answer. Just the whistling wind. A strong gust buffeted me, I lost my footing, and fell.

It was like a slow-motion disaster. I was screaming-

No! No! No!

My hands shifted out in front of me far too slowly and darkness swallowed me up.

OH THE HORROR...THE HORROR

I woke up rubbing my head. My hand came away wet and sticky. Low light, thick condensation, and blurry vision all conspired against me, but it looked like blood. I was lying prone on something hard. Rock, I assumed. Groaning, I rose to a seated position.

It was some sort of subterranean tunnel. A steady drip resounded and a pale glow emanated through the pervading mist. My legs felt hard and cold, but they were responsive enough for me to ascend into a squat. A moist coolness cloistered in around me, and I shivered under my leathers. I couldn't feel the tips of my fingers. My gloves were gone, and I peered around, trying to see in the low illumination.

Far above, a thin blue light glimmered. Long stalactites drooped down, their edges glistening with a sheen of water. I imagined a million creepy, slimy things from my childhood terrors. Peering around desperately, anxiety washed over me. My teeth were chattering, my skin breaking out in goose bumps, but I lurched forward. My right leg hurt, and somehow, I'd managed to jar my spine. Stabs of pain shot up as I moved. A soft hiss echoed, and I froze. Standing absolutely still for several minutes, the sound didn't recur, and all I could hear was distant water dripping. I edged forward slowly, my hands desperately probing ahead. Absolute blackness swallowed me up.

The dripping grew louder as I kept moving, my slow pace maddening as my feet started to slosh in something liquid. A slowly intensifying tone grew into a nauseating, high pitched drone. I shook my head, but nothing abated. I started to feel dizzy. The air felt charged.

A pale speck of light manifested in the distance.

Sunlight! There must be a way out!

I fought the urge to dash forward. The water had risen to the top of my feet now, slowing my progress and seeping into my shoes. Something struck my foot, and I froze. Maybe it was just a rock. It didn't feel like a rock, but I was scaring myself more than I needed. I just had to keep moving. Something hit my foot again, this time near the ankle, and I broke into a run.

The speck progressed into an oblong portal. My heart was pounding, my nerves on fire, and I poured every ounce of energy I had into my legs, It didn't feel like enough. My boots were too heavy, my thick trousers and a heavy coat all conspiring against me.

Fuck it.

I wriggled out of my coat and left it behind. I knew I'd regret that later, but nothing would matter if I was dead!

The passageway grew larger, and the floor curved up into an ankle high mound of rock. I cleared it with a sailing leap, tumbling back down onto a sandy stretch of stone. My leg screamed in pain, and I almost lost control, but I managed to steady myself and grind to a halt.

White light bathed me. I staggered left, then right, blinking my eyes and trying to get some bearing. The distorting flashes in my vision faded, and I could see that I was in some large subterranean chamber. Jutting out of the sand nearby was a chunk of stone, the top bulging in strange, artificial patterns. I scooped it up and raised it to eye level. It resembled an ancient fossil, but not of any creature I was familiar with. The thing was thick and wormlike, it's segmented body curling from a pointy tail into a much larger head harboring long, thin teeth. I dropped the fossil and looked around.

On the right the sand rose into a small hill topped by a smooth black strip that looked to perfect to be natural. I wandered over, starting to feel the cold and already regretting ditching the jacket. As I ascended, the sand dropped away at the apex into a wide, rectangular hole. I peered in and a rush of cold, harshened by a metallic bite, wafted up to greet me. I jerked back. It seemed to emanate something else as well. Something inhuman.

Maybe I was over thinking this, the strangeness of yesterday coloring my vision. I dug in my pocket, pulled out my Maglite, and peered into the depths. I couldn't make out much, Smooth, black walls spiraled into a sandy floor. I knew I was going to regret this, but I had to check it out. Besides, I rationalized, it might be the best way out of here.

A short drop, and I landed on a downward slope. I almost slid, correcting my descent by flailing my arms and dramatically shifting my weight. Holding the light aloft, I traipsed into the depths.

The floor started to be ridged in patterns far too symmetrical to be natural. The ebony tops glimmered under my flashlight. A musky, earthen smell wafted through, it's density almost suffocating. There was a strange, static charge in the air, and it lifted the small hairs on my body. It was noticeably colder down here as well, and I was starting to shiver even more. I couldn't shake the uncomfortable feeling of something else present, and this long downward trail was starting to feel like a really bad idea.

My beam caught a dark opening on the right and I slowed my approach. It was a small room, harboring a few large rectangular boxes. A transparent dome topped each box, a convoluted mass of petrified tubes swarming into the foundation.

What the fuck was this?

I slowed as I ventured in, my beam holding steady on the strange boxes. Up close they looked like coffins. Something gleamed beneath the clouded cover. I stepped up to the edge and pointed my light in. Something dark and slick was all that was visible. I swiveled my beam back and forth, but a crusty layer of film coated the insides of the cover, and I couldn't make out anything clearly. Peering around the edges, I looked for some kind of seem. This was feeling like a terrible idea... but the curiosity was too great. I promised myself I would have a quick look and then make a hasty exit. I could always come back later for a more thorough investigation.

Finding a few protrusions on the side I gently and tapped one. It didn't move. Clasping the tail end of the flashlight between my teeth, I reached over and grasped the other protrusion. Tucking my fingers underneath I pulled up. With a low hiss the lid cracked open. I wriggled my fingers under the lip. It was moist and a little sticky, the heavy edges digging into my arm. Saliva was starting to pool in my mouth from holding the flashlight and threatening to overflow in a trail of drool. I transferred one hand to the light and lifted up with the other. With a soft crack, the lid broke free and tumbled over.

The liquid inside was the color of oil. Raised bumps that resembled fish skin broke the surface in a few spots. I twisted the beam toward the top of the container. A roundish mound protruded slightly from the liquid, the top sinking into two parallel holes. It reminded me of something—a face? A very strange face if it was, but the oily liquid obscured all the features.

This could be the find of the century! I need to get some archeologists down here stat! First the book, and now this!

Come to think of it, where was the book? I must have dropped it when I fell...

Then the depressions opened up and two bright orange eyes glared out at me. I jumped back.

"Fuck! "

I directed the beam back in the box.

Was I seeing things?

Nothing. Just the oily black mound. Backing up a few feet, I circled around until I was on the opposite side. Leaning over, I gently pulled the lid back on. It sealed with a low hiss. I rolled the beam over the lid, looking for any movement. But there was nothing.

Every nerve was on end.

I had better leave... now!

Just as I was turning, twin specks of orange emerged again. I ran, almost diving out of the chamber, and stumbled madly back the way I had come.

The ground was slippery, the upward ascent conspired against me, and I kept falling, skinning my palms. But I was finally returned to the initial chamber and once again was bathed in sunlight. Cupping my hands over my eyes, I tried desperately to regain focus. Peering around desperately, I broke into a run towards the only opening I saw.

I must have been getting deeper, because water started to trickle down the sidewalls and accumulate on the floor. The path was growing slick, and I wiped out, my feet shooting out from under me as I landed heavily on my side. Cursing, I scrambled back up, pain scorching my left leg as an arc of agony shot up my right.

Goddamnit!

I hobbled along, the sting slowing my pace into a loping gait.

I had to stop... for a minute at least. The wall was slightly hollowed out just ahead, and I lumbered forward, dropping heavily into the shallow cavity. My breath was coming fast and furious, cloaking me in a hazy mist of condensation. My small light couldn't make it past the steam, and I felt blind. I held my breath, pressing my hand against my heart to muffle the crazed beating, and listened intently. But no sound came to me. Other than the tribal pounding in my head.

Was there anything pursuing me?

I threw the arc of my beam up and down the corridor. The watery floor shimmered and I thought I saw movement when something eel-like quickly wriggled out of sight.

Do eels even live down here?

A sharp stab in the lower back nearly sent me flying forward. Desperately scraping under my shirt, my hand grasped a slimy appendage. It was squirming wildly, and as I tightened my grip, even sharper pain stabbed in. I could feel my skin stretching, followed by a release and the cold flush of blood. Followed by another intense pain as it bit into my hand.

Fuck! Fuck!

I swung my hand out and shook it fiercely. A long, black thing, resembling a giant leech but sporting a shining array of pin-like teeth, was latched on. I slammed it into the wall, and it bit deeper. I cried out and slammed it even harder. Again, and again. The grip loosened, and I managed to pull it off. It wriggled ferociously in my hand, the formidable teeth gnashing savagely. I slung it as far down the passageway as I could, ducked out of the alcove, and started running again. Now the new pain in my back and hand added to the sting from the fall. A chorus of agony, making every footfall torture.

I could hear a splashing behind me, growing ever closer, and I broke out in tears of frustration.

Fuck! Fuck! Fuck!

Just as I was on the verge of being overwhelmed, the ground shifted upward sharply, the passageway dried up, and the noises receded.

I didn't dare stop, but I slowed, my failing body crying out more by the minute. The path was growing steeper, and I was in too much pain to stay upright. Falling to my knees, I tried to crawl up with my fingers. The walls drew closer, and claustrophobia started to set in. Every part of my body seemed to hurt. My breathing was rapid and shallow, and the confines so close I couldn't even turn around. I was starting to freak out. I ground to a halt and tried to calm myself. I didn't want to keep ascending, but I was far too terrified of what lay below to head back down. A sliver of light flickered overhead.

Was that sunlight?

I forgot how exhausted I was for a moment, and rabidly scrambled forward. The light grew brighter... I was sure it was sunlight!

I scraped upward, through an ever-narrower gap. As I started to get stuck, my claustrophobia kicked in. I was panicking and had to close my eyes and try to gain some control.

A couple minutes passed, and I felt I had dropped from red alert to maybe orange. Mustering my strength again, wriggling and squirming as my pants got caught in rock, I finally managed to free myself. A draft of freezing air hit me, and something fluttered by.

Snow? Was I that high up?

Worming my hand up past my head, skinning my knuckles in the process, I threw them over a slight outcropping and pulled with all my might. My body moved a few inches, but my boots were stuck. I twisted them one way, then another, and managed to advance a few more inches. I was starting to freak out again. Summoning all my strength, I threw it into a gut-wrenching thrust, my fingertips shooting back arcs of pain as I pulled with everything I had.

My foot twisted painfully, and I popped out, erupting from the cloistered darkness and into a blinding landscape of snow. A fierce wind beat at my face, my arms and fingers were already half lifeless from the constant chill, and this only made it worse. Mucus clogged my throat, and watery snot rolled down my upper lip. I swiped at my nose and managed only to spread the salty wetness around, throwing blood into the mix as my nose made contact with my torn hand. I felt something cold and damp against my stomach and peered down. A thick swatch of blood stained my shirt. Apparently, the wound hadn't sealed. A trail dribbled out, tarnishing the white snow with drops of crimson. I was beaten down, worn out, and seriously doubted I could make it back to civilization alive. A soft humming reverberated, followed by a violent eruption from behind.

I was thrown face first into the snow. My eardrums popped, and I twisted around to see that the cave was now glowing. Then, the entire upper mountainside above crumbled. Chunks of rock and snow poured down the sides and I twisted as, miraculously, the avalanche of debris rolled past.

The noise intensified, and I clapped my hands over my ears. And then... what happened might have been an illusion—or maybe I was going mad—but a giant black disc rose out of the mountaintop. Pinpricks of light dotting its convex belly, it hovered in place for a moment. Then it flew forward, growing mammoth in size and drowning me in shadow as it passed.

I sat utterly still, in complete shock, until a brisk gust stirred me from my reverie. From this elevation, I could see the tall buildings of a town not far off. Inverness, I assumed. The giant disc was suspended overhead. It looked like something out of a bad sci-fi movie. I shook my head and rubbed my eyes then dared to look again. The mammoth disc started to rotate. Slowly at first but picking up speed until a giant flash resonated from its belly and a concussive force slammed me backwards.

The wind knocked out of me, I crawled upright, gasping for breath. Just as I started to suck in air, I stood up and looked back in the direction of the city. But there was no city. Just the giant disc, blocking out the sinking sun.

BLOOD AND SNOW

My head was pounding. I felt nauseous and weak. And cold... so cold. Life was draining out of me, step by step. The wound on my back had swollen and now it felt huge and numb. My hands were losing color and feeling. I wanted to sit down, just let it all end. But I couldn't. There was horror yet to come.

Life is indeed comic... but the joke is on mankind. -HP Lovecraf

ABOUT THE AUTHOR

At 18, I was kicked out of my house. I spent the next 8 months homeless, sometimes sleeping in the woods.

Finally getting a steady job and a place to live, my friend flipped my beat-up old car, and I went through the windshield.

After a two-week recovery, I moved from Northern Virginia to downtown Washington DC and in with my girlfriend. A year and a half later, a crackhead broke into the house.

A knife fight with him severed the tendon on my left hand. After surgery and yet another move, I finally attended art school. My work made it into galleries, political cartoons for Madcap Magazine, covers for Maximum Rock and Roll, and numerous t-shirts and ads. I left art school early, on the advice of my teacher, for a career in NYC.

Interviews with DC Comics and Marvel made me realize they paid very little, and only wanted me to draw superheroes.

A year later, at the urging of a tattoo artist, I went into the field. I have now been tattooing for 24 years. I've been featured in a slew of books, magazines, newspapers, and on TV in the US and Europe, both for my tattoo work, and my traditional art. Tattooing has been very good to me. Life, not so much. I've had brain cancer, was in Bellevue when the twin towers went down, and six years later, my wife died in a hit and run.

But life is what you make of it. This is my first novel and four more have followed. I now do art for books, magazines, host a podcast entitled Skull Session with Dan Henk, and own a tattoo shop. Check out all my latest work on my website at danhenk.com and follow me on Facebook and Instagram @danhenkauthor.